# Heaven Sent

## PADDLE CREEK COLLEGE
### BOOK ONE

**HJ WELCH**

Heaven Sent
Paddle Creek College Book One

Copyright © 2022 by HJ Welch

Cover Design by Cate Ashwood

# CHAPTER 1

## *Seth*

MY ASS IS ONE OF MY BEST FEATURES, OKAY? IT DIDN'T NEED
the figurative kicking it just got out on the field, and it
*damned* well doesn't need a literal knocking to the ground
right now.

But I have little choice in the matter as about two
hundred and fifty pounds of pure muscle comes flying into
me with an excitable bellow, like a wrecking ball with the
temperament of a puppy dog.

"What the actual *fuck,* Quinn?" I yell as I try and push my
most irritating teammate off me and roll away. But the big
lug is determinedly hugging me on the grass outside of the
Paddle Creek College stadium. I groan and accept that until
Marty Quinn wants to let me go, I'm probably stuck.

That's why he's the linebacker and I'm the (star) quarterback.

I drop my head and watch a gaggle of excitable fans of
our rival team ambling across the grass, foam fingers in
Albertson University's signature red-and-gold colors held
high in the air. Guilt washes through me again. Our fans
aren't celebrating tonight. There's no worse feeling than

knowing people trusted you and you let them down, especially so early on in the season. *Fuck.*

"Seth!" Quinn cries in delight as he finally rocks back and releases me. "You looked like you needed some loving, bro."

I grit my teeth and ruffle my hair as I sit back up. If I'm going to be embarrassed even further in front of dozens of people, I might as well look good. I'm just thankful that the majority of the spectators will have left by now, and there are mostly just stragglers lingering.

"Your idea of cheering me up after Albertson creamed us is to beat the shit out of me?" I ask with a raised eyebrow.

At least he has the decency to look sheepish. He rubs the back of his neck. "I did shout 'Surprise hug!' but maybe you didn't hear me."

I sigh and ignore the curious looks from the last people trickling out of the stadium as I brush my jeans and stand up. I can tell they're our fans from the teal and purple they're wearing, and I try not to feel too ashamed. There's still an aroma of fried food and hot dogs in the air as well as smoke from the fireworks. In the distance, cheery pop music is playing from a loudspeaker, the bass notes traveling to where we're standing.

God, this guy irritates me. The rest of my teammates had the good sense to leave me to my thunderous mood after that humiliating defeat. But three years on the Paddle Creek Panthers together and it's still all just a big joke to Marty Quinn.

It's not a joke to me. This is my life. This is *serious*.

"Don't you care that we just lost?" I ask as he hauls his huge frame up. He's in good shape—I've seen what he can bench press. Whereas where I'm lean and fast, he's built like a fucking tank.

He shrugs as he dusts his hands. "Yeah, but you played good, bro. *Real* good. That last touchdown you made was—"

He makes a chef's kiss motion.

I know I should take it as a compliment, but all it does is drag my mood down further. Football is about all this podunk town has going for it. Saturday nights is about the only time it truly comes alive. And when we lose, it's like the people here aren't sure what'll get them through the weekend after that.

"It still wasn't good enough, though, was it?" I say.

"No, it wasn't," a third voice cuts into our conversation.

I roll my eyes, what little is left of my patience evaporating.

"McKenna," I say stiffly, crossing my arms as I turn to face him and a couple of his usual insipid cronies. Quinn also moves to look at the richest and most arrogant prick in our class, a frown on my teammate's usually goofy face.

"Not everything's all about football, bro," he says quietly.

Logan McKenna rolls his eyes. Part of me has to agree with him. Pretty much everything I do in life is oriented toward football. But then he opens his smirking mouth, and that's when our brief allyship fades.

"Uh, it is when your family's *name* is going to be on the damned building."

I scoff. "Not yet, daddy's boy."

He smooths down his blazer and gives me a once-over. Whatever, dude. I know his folks basically own this town, and he thinks I'm white trash. Over the last decade or so, the McKennas have been buying up businesses left, right, and center, apparently. The thing is, Albertson is the town that gets all the county funding in these parts. Money attracts money, right? Word is that the McKennas thought they could make an easy splash here in Paddle Creek. But they never actually *invest* in anything. They just own it, so everything stays run down and out of date.

That doesn't stop Logan McKenna from thinking he's the

fucking shit, though. I wouldn't care what this prick thinks about me if his dad didn't have so much sway over the booster club and the Board of Regents. They control the Panthers' funding, and everyone knows boosters have a behind-closed-doors say on who stays on the team.

If they don't like the star quarterback anymore, then chances are they'll bench him and bring the second string in.

I'm already regretting my quip back, but not enough to apologize. I was in a foul enough mood before this dick popped up to rile me further.

"You're right," McKenna says smoothly. "The name change hasn't been finalized. And if you boys keep playing like a bunch of pussies instead of panthers, maybe we'll take our funding elsewhere. To Albertson, perhaps?"

I curl my lip and shake my head, apparently unable to stop my mouth from shooting off. "You McKennas would rather be big fish in a little pond than compete with the head honchos over at Albertson. You're not going anywhere."

Quinn tries to deescalate the situation, and steps between us with his arms raised. "Hey, guys, can we just—" But McKenna doesn't seem to be intimidated by the man twice his size, probably because he knows that Quinn is about as tough as a marshmallow off the field. He and his cronies just step around the man mountain to jab his finger at me, his eyes blazing.

"I'm pretty sure it's *you* that's not going anywhere, Eisen," McKenna spits triumphantly at me.

For a second, I'm not sure what he's talking about. It's long enough to notice that someone has stopped and is watching our exchange from a dozen or so feet away. *Shit.* It's some little nerd, judging by the couple of books he's hugging to his chest and heavy-looking backpack. He's even got gold-framed glasses on his cute nose to complete the geek aesthetic. In fact...damn. This kid is fucking *adorable.* If we were down at the Ice Cream Parlor in town, I'd have gotten his number immediately and already be making plans to worship his pretty ass as soon as possible.

Instead, he's witnessing this dumpster fire of an altercation. How long has he been watching? Did he see Quinn slam me into the ground? Urgh, could this evening get any worse?

I really, *really* shouldn't have thought that.

"What are you talking about?" I demand of McKenna. I don't understand how his retort is the insult he clearly thinks it is. I'm graduating next semester and then I'll never have to see his smug face again.

He quirks an eyebrow and shrugs casually. "Oh, just something a little birdie told me. Not been keeping an eye on your credits, have you, Eisen? You know you'll need an extra four next semester to graduate, don't you?"

My blood runs cold. "You've been snooping around in my files?"

He laughs and flicks his blazer back so he can slip his hands into the pockets of his jeans, which probably cost more than my whole wardrobe put together. "Really not the point, but what else should I expect from a meathead? One too many concussions, I bet."

"Hey, that's not funny," Quinn snaps, looming to his full height. "Guys can get really fucked up from injuries like that."

McKenna scoffs. "No one's *making* you play this uncivilized sport. You can't whine when you get a little knocked around."

"Actually," a delicate voice pipes up, but there's a hint of something ferocious there as well. "Most of the Panthers are on athletic scholarships. So they *do* have to play if they want their degree. It's either that or the ROTC for a lot of them if they want higher education."

My eyebrows crawl up my forehead as I slowly turn around. Quinn does as well, and we discover the little nerd who was watching before. Except now he's crept closer, and he's clinging to his books as he trembles. With fear or rage, I can't tell.

"Wha—" I utter, but our nerdy defender isn't done.

"They've got more talent in one pinky than you have in your whole body, Logan. At least their fathers didn't *buy* their way into college."

Quinn's jaw drops. "Whoa, buddy," he says, sounding amused.

Unnervingly, McKenna doesn't appear all that fazed.

"None of that matters if you don't have enough credits to graduate. I heard some big scouts were sniffing around you, Eisen. Shame. No team wants a quarterback who flunked out or can't graduate." He snaps his head. "And I don't know what you're guffawing about, Quinn. Your GPA is atrocious, and they won't pay for you to come back another year."

Quinn's face falls. "It's not *that* bad," he mumbles.

McKenna's grin is savage. "Oh, yeah, it is. You'll both be gone before we even get to graduation, just a blip on this college's radar as my family *finally* does something to turn it around. How sad. Imagine peaking at twenty-two. It's all downhill from here, guys."

His cronies laugh almost as if on command, and I wonder if any of them have had an original thought in their lives. Everyone knows they just hang around with Logan to bask in that McKenna glory and wealth. Because for every penny they don't spend on this town, you can bet they hoard it for themselves. Personally, you couldn't pay me to put up with his shit.

But that's beside the point. I think my brain is spiraling and latching on to random thoughts to avoid the real issue at hand.

I mean…I knew my grades were a little light, but have I really not taken enough classes?

"If I'm missing credits, then I'll just make them up," I say. I know I should just walk away, but this prick has me on the defense and I feel like I have to stand up for myself. "Just because we lost today doesn't mean I'm off course to go pro." I shake my head. "Your jealousy is pathetic, man. Our friend here is right. What the hell have you ever achieved in your life that your daddy didn't pay for?"

I glance at the little nerd who fucking beams at me. His face lights up almost as much as his golden, cherub-like hair under the floodlights illuminating the stadium. Something flip-flops in my chest, and I vow that no matter how shitty this exchange gets, I'm not letting him leave without getting his number. The way he stood up to McKenna took guts, man.

"You don't have the time," McKenna says gleefully. "Neither of you. It's going to be soooo sweet seeing you get the boot. I bet they'll do it this semester before the championships. Maybe they'll promote someone *worthy* to take the field."

He looks between me and Quinn, who seems kind of shell-shocked. Not me. Oh, no. I'm pissed.

I see what's going on here.

"This is about your buddy Perkins," I say, the pieces finally falling into place. "You want me off the team so he can take my place!"

Perkins is one of those guys whose arrogance writes checks his talent can't cash. He's a third-rate player at best. But he's in McKenna's inner circle, and that's who they probably came here to meet. Not that he's here now to confront me himself. No, of course he's letting his buddies do his dirty work for him.

Naturally, McKenna wants me out to give that douchebag a shot. Come to think of it, he probably used whatever contacts he has in the school's offices to get access to my files. I'm not sure why he's going for Quinn as well. Maybe just opportunity, since he happens to be here? Whatever. He doesn't care about any of this, not really. But *me?*

"Fuck you, McKenna," I growl. "I'll give up my position when and only when I graduate, so suck it."

"No thanks." McKenna laughs. "We all know where that cock's been. Anyway—I'll believe it when I see you in a cap and gown. In fact, I'd bet you a thousand bucks you flake out before then."

His buddies get a real laugh out of that, but I grit my teeth and see red.

"Deal," I snap.

"Whoa, Seth, wait a sec," Quinn says, but all that does is draw McKenna's attention back to him.

"You and Quinn," he says with a jerk of his thumb. "You both have to walk that stage or pay up."

"Hey, no," Quinn cries. "Leave me out of it!"

"Deal," I repeat. I've got tunnel vision from my rage, and I'm not backing down. Besides, if I get signed, that'll be chump change. "We each pay you a grand if we fail. But if we graduate, then you have to pay us each a thousand crisp dollar bills."

"Ha!" McKenna crows. "Easy money. You'll never do it."

"Yes, they will!"

For the second time that evening, I'm compelled to turn and look at our little nerd in surprise, only to see him quivering with rage and determination.

"Will they, now?" McKenna mocks him as he steps toward him. I immediately inch closer to his side, and I notice Quinn does as well. Like suddenly, we're his bodyguards. "How do you know that?"

The smaller guy visibly swallows and looks up at me and Quinn. I've got to say I'm impressed at his faith in us, but as determined as I am to whoop McKenna's ass, I'm not sure how founded that faith is.

"Because I'm tutoring them," the little guy blurts out, his cheeks going red. "And I've got one of the highest GPAs in my entire class. So you better be prepared to pay up!"

McKenna's laugh is incredulous and cruel.

"Oh, you want to play, four eyes? Fine. But not without any skin in the game. Same terms for you. A thousand bucks."

The little cutie's face rapidly drains of all color, and I wave my hand between them both. His offer was thoughtful, but I don't expect him to actually go through with it, especially not with real money on the line.

Well, real money to us right now. It's Monopoly money to McKenna, and I won't let him draw someone innocent into his stupid game.

"Hey, no—" I try and intervene, but I'm interrupted.

And not by Mckenna or Quinn like I expected.

"Deal!" the little nerd cries. "Seth and Marty both graduate, and you'll pay us each a thousand dollars."

He thrusts his small, trembling hand out toward McKenna.

I share a glance with Quinn, but before we can interject, McKenna grabs it and shakes.

"Deal," he snarls.

What the fuck just happened?

# CHAPTER 2

*Gabe*

WHAT IN THE NAME OF THE GODS HAVE I JUST GOTTEN MYSELF into?

Logan McKenna smirks as he slides his hand out of mine, making me shiver—the bad kind. "I guess I'll be seeing you boys around, then," he says before he and his friends turn and walk away, chuckling among themselves.

"What the ever-loving shit just happened?" Marty Quinn cries out. Usually, he's so cheerful and positive. It makes me wince to hear the anger in his voice.

I also turn around to look at him and Seth Eisen, my pulse quickening. In the moment, my blood was pumping, and I was just so *mad* I'm not sure I had full control of the words that were coming out of my mouth.

But I really did say that I was already tutoring both of them. So…does that mean I'm now *actually* tutoring them? We each have a thousand dollars on the line, after all.

It appears I'm not the only one who hasn't forgotten that.

"I don't have that kind of money, bro!" Marty cries in distress at Seth. I feel him. Neither do I. But my stupid pride managed to forget that in the thick of it.

"It's going to be okay," Seth says, fanning his palms like he's calming a wild horse.

"How?" Marty demands. "I already knew there was a chance I wasn't going to make up the grades in time to graduate. I'd made peace with that. But I need every penny I've got to get on my feet after I leave—diploma or not. My family can't support me any more than they already have!"

"Well, I *haven't* made peace with not graduating!" Seth yells. "McKenna is right. They could pull me from the team and screw my chances of going pro! I know this is all fun and games to you, but football *means* something to me. It's my ticket out of here!"

"Um, excuse me?" I say, raising my hand like I'm still in high school. But I can't blame myself for being nervous. When they both turn their attention to me, my insides go all hot and liquidy, and it takes me a second to remember what the hell I wanted to say.

Oh, yeah.

"I can actually tutor you. I'm doing pretty much all your courses, and I wasn't kidding. I'm here on an academic scholarship and I'm really good at what I do."

Seth raises an eyebrow, making me all squirmy. He's fit and lean and a couple of inches taller than me. Marty, on the other hand, is bulky and a couple of inches taller than *Seth,* so he towers over me. His muscles aren't as defined as Seth's, as they're hidden under a nice soft layer. Seth's abs could cut fucking glass.

Uh…yeah. So I've seen them both topless. Many times. In photos and in real life. I might be a geek, but I also really do like football. I haven't missed a game since I arrived in Paddle Creek, and, well, I might follow a lot of the team members' Instagram accounts.

A boy can daydream, right?

Except this isn't a dream anymore. Eisen and Quinn—

local legends—are currently giving me their undivided attention.

"But…you're a freshman?" Seth says dubiously.

I give him a little one-armed shrug. These books I'm holding are starting to get pretty heavy, but I'm not going to interrupt this conversation for *anything.*

"A lot of it is about knowing how to write essays and interpret the text. You're liberal arts majors, right?" I ask like I don't already know. They both nod, and I smile. "Me, too. I specialize in classics—ancient Greek mythology. Latin. Stuff like that. I really love all the Greek gods, and, um, yeah. I'm doing as many electives as I can. I might not know your specific courses, but I'm sure I could help you study the living daylights out of them. I mean, if you want."

"Aww, that's so nice of you, bud," Marty says, clapping my shoulder so hard I almost stagger off my feet. "But I couldn't ask you to give up all that time."

"And I really couldn't pay you," Seth adds before looking at Marty. "I don't have the money, either. Believe me. Not unless—until—I get signed."

I'm already shaking my head, though.

"I wouldn't expect you to pay me," I assure them both. "And I know I'm a massive loser, but I'd get a real kick out of studying senior syllabus stuff." I try not to blush or stutter over my next words. "And it would be pretty, um, cool to help out two of Paddle Creek's star athletes. It would, um, be my honor, actually."

I'm so embarrassed by the time I stop talking that I have to glance away. But then I glimpse Marty grinning and placing his hands on his hips, puffing out his chest. "We are pretty famous and awesome, I guess. Right, bro?"

Seth rolls his eyes. Their rivalry on and off the field is pretty well known. From what I can tell, Marty likes to play a lot of jokes and games, but Seth seems so serious and kind of scary. He is the quarterback and the team captain, after all. There's definitely friction between the two players, but when Seth turns back to look at me, it feels like there's a real warmth there that totally makes me melt.

I must be imagining it, though, right? He's just being nice to a silly freshman.

"I won't lie. If the situation is as bad as McKenna is making it out to be, I absolutely won't say no to getting some help. Why don't I take your number, and then I can let you know when I've investigated further?"

He pulls out his phone and raises his eyebrows. Before I can process that *Seth Eisen is asking for my actual phone number,* Marty huffs and puffs and also yanks out his cell.

"Well, uh, yeah. Same, bro. I'll take you up on your very kind and generous offer."

Seth glares at him. "You don't care about graduating. Why are you trying to poach my tutor?"

Marty shakes his head and waves his phone in my direction. "Nuh-*uh.* Just because I thought I wasn't going to graduate doesn't mean I don't *want* to! I didn't think I, like, had any options. But now I do with my main man here!" His face falls. "Oh, bro. My bad. I don't even know your name."

Seth's face falls as well, obviously realizing he never asked either. But it's cool. I don't mind. Why *would* they know who I am? They're basically Paddle Creek royalty and I'm some lowly commoner who I still can't even believe they're talking to.

"It's fine," I say genuinely, but my laugh is a bit nervous. Like I'm being audacious even telling them who I am. "Um, my name's Gabriel Visoth. Or Gabe. I'm Gabe. It's really nice to meet you both."

Marty pulls me into a crushing hug and ruffles my hair. "Real nice to meet you too, bro. You were super brave standing up to Mr. Moneybags Douchebag." He frowns and releases me. "That's too many 'bags.' See! That's why I need a tutor!"

Seth tuts and sticks out his hand for me to shake. He's got such a strong grip. "Nice to meet you, Gabe. Now let me get your digits. I've taken up enough of your time tonight."

I want to tell him that this is the most amazing and exciting thing that's happened to me since I got to college, but I don't want to come across as a sycophant. So I just rattle off my number and watch in amusement as both guys try to compete as to who can input it into their phones faster.

"Give it up, Quinn," Seth says with a scowl. "Gabe only has so much time, and I *need* this."

"So do I!" Marty replies indignantly, shoving his phone into his jeans pocket. "I'm not wasting the last three years if I don't have to! I'll be the first person in my whole family to graduate college, and I got a *lot* of family."

"Then maybe you should have studied harder," Seth fires back.

"Seriously," I say, waving my hands at them. "Guys. It's fine. I can tutor you both at the same time, so it won't eat into my schedule all that much."

They don't seem to hear me.

"Me?" Marty cries. "You're just as fucked as I am, bro. I might have missed some papers because I didn't understand the questions or—y'know—whatever. But you didn't take enough credits! All you had to do was read the little page thingy on the internet that helped you add them up!"

"Guys," I plead, but they're squaring up with each other like they've already forgotten about me.

"Because I'm dedicated to the *team,*" Seth snarls. "Who cares about Shakesbeard or whatever when I've got plays to run and drills to devise? The team relies on me. This *town* relies on me. All you do is goof off. Why aren't I surprised that you're a slacker in class as well?"

"GUYS!"

"You don't know me, man," Marty says, jabbing his finger into Seth's chest. Seth angrily bats it away.

"Don't touch me."

"I'm not a slacker," Marty says defiantly. There's a tiny break in his voice that I hear, but I'm not sure Seth does. That word hurt Marty, I'm sure.

"Then why do you need tutoring?"

"Why do you?"

"That's IT!"

They finally look at me, quiet again. There aren't many people around anymore, and it suddenly feels very still and silent. I take a couple of breaths, trying to stop myself from trembling, my face from getting hot, or my eyes filling with tears.

I'm pretty sure I fail at all three. But I hate fighting so much, especially from two guys I practically worship.

Squeezing my fists, I resolve myself and look between them both. "I'll either tutor you together at the same time or not at all. We all got into this mess, so we're all going to get out of it. As a *team.*"

I know it's a low blow, but I shoot that last word at Seth like it's a javelin. However, I'm sure it's the only way to get through to him what needs to happen. Teams are something he cares about.

I'm not leaving Marty behind.

And I'm not losing a thousand dollars.

I can't quite believe my gumption, though, as I point my finger at them both, juggling my books in one arm. They feel like lead, they're so heavy now, but I hold on just a little longer.

"You have my number. Let me know if you want to quit.

Otherwise, I'll see you tomorrow at the library at ten o'clock." I spin on my heel, pause, then spin around again. "Unless that's not a convenient time for either of you. In which case, text me and let me know a better time. *Or* if you're going to quit. Otherwise, I'll, um, be at the library."

This time I really do turn and stomp away, biting my lip and forcing myself not to tumble into a panic attack.

I've said my piece.

"Athena, grant me wisdom," I whisper pitifully, hugging my books and glancing up to the sky, like she might be able to help me.

Whatever happens now is in the hands of the gods.

# CHAPTER 3

## Marty

FUCKING FUCKING *FUCK!* THIS IS WHAT PEOPLE MEAN WHEN they say that thing about doing a nice thing, then bad stuff happening anyway!

No good deed goes unpunished. That's it. My pops likes saying that a lot. I always thought it was an excuse not to help out others, which isn't like him, so it always confused me. But right now, I'm wishing I'd listened to him just a little harder.

All I'd wanted to do was cheer Seth up! He was so sad after we lost, even though there are like ninety other guys on the team. It wasn't his fault. He played like a champ! I've got three brothers and two sisters, and we were always taught that a bit of rough and tumble was the best way to get out of a funk. So when I saw him, I didn't think. I just ran in for a bear hug.

I should know better by now, though. No matter what I do, it seems like I never fail to irritate him. That guts me, y'know? He's such a great guy. So talented and cool and hot as fuck. I just wish we could be friends.

I'd say we'll be graduating soon, and therefore, that boat

has probably sailed. But it turns out we might *not* even be graduating at all! This is fucked up.

That cute kid—Gabe, he said his name was—offered to help us. But now I'm watching him walk away, all pissed off and hurt because Seth and I were fighting over him.

"Shit," I say as he gets smaller and smaller in the dark, leaving the glow of the floodlights.

"If you'd have just left me alone, none of this would have happened," Seth grumbles.

"Then you wouldn't know about your credits," I shoot back. I point at where Gabe vanished. "That little cutie offered to help us both. Are you really so selfish that you'd screw us both over if you can't keep him all to yourself?"

He narrows his eyes at me. "Are we talking about dating or tutoring here?"

I scowl and try not to get flustered. I mean, yeah, I've got eyes. He's adorable, and I have a sneaky suspicion he doesn't even know it. I'd totally take him out on a date and romance the shit out of him. But that *isn't* actually what we're discussing right now.

"Tutoring," I say, pulling a face like 'duh.' "I just called him cute cuz he's cute. But he's not going to be anything if you're going to scare him off and fuck us both over."

Seth sighs and rubs his forehead. "Fine," he says eventually, then points a finger at me. "But you better not goof around on this. I mean it. We work hard, we kick ass on the field, we graduate, and we get paid. That's it."

"Sure," I say, sticking out my hand. Everybody seems to want to shake on this, so now it's my turn. "I'm going to be the best study buddy. You'll see."

He hums and squeezes my hand before withdrawing. "I guess I will see. Night, Quinn."

I watch as he saunters off into the night, taking a second to sit with my thoughts. I have a lot of them right now. But after a while, I realize that my chest is sorta warm and full, and I think it's hope I'm feeling. Yeah, I was kinda wishing that if I ignored the grades situation things might work out on their own. Dumb, I know. But school stuff has never been a strength of mine. Gabe was right. I totally only got into college because I made it onto the football team, and I'm okay with that.

But if I could *actually* graduate…man. My folks will lose it, they'll be so proud.

And so what if I'm also excited that I'm really going to be hanging out with Seth friggin' Eisen finally. Being on the team doesn't count. I'm not sure we've even had a proper conversation bro-on-bro-like that didn't involve defense formations or protein diet tips or whatever.

I've tried getting his attention so many times with the kind of crazy stunts I get a kick out of pulling. Like the time I put Jell-O in Dukey's shoes or drew on Ozo's face when he fell asleep on the bus. Most of the guys think I'm hilarious, but not Seth.

This could be my chance to finally get through to him—maybe. I could just be asking for disappointment. But beneath all that grumpiness, he does seem like a nice guy. I love the way he cares *so* much about the team and our fans. He never wants to let anyone down.

It's funny, but back in freshman year, when we all started out, I kind of had a crush on him. However, he then made it pretty clear he thinks I'm nothing more than the team clown, so I let those feelings go.

I don't expect any of that to change now. It's not like the clouds are going to part and he's going to be all 'Dude! You're my bro!' y'know? But when we go our separate ways from Paddle Creek, I'd like to think we were kind of buddies.

And then there's this new cutie, Gabe, to consider. I play back everything he said as I start wandering toward the trolley stop so I can grab a streetcar into town. The way he stood up to Logan McKenna made me think of one of those adorable little dogs that look like caramel-colored clouds when they bark to defend their owners. Like, that's not going to do much, my little dude, but damn I'm impressed you tried.

He had such pretty lips, as well. I bet he's a good kisser. He seemed so shy, but…

Wait—*no!* He's going to be my tutor. *Our* tutor—mine and Seth's. I can't think of him like that. But hell, I've definitely got sex on the brain now. I'm always horny after games. I think it's the adrenaline. It's probably why my feet are automatically taking me to Creams.

The Ice Cream Parlor, as it's officially known is the best gay bar north of Indianapolis. That's about all Paddle Creek has going for it. Creams and the Panthers. We get people coming from all over the state as well as Illinois and Ohio, so there are always tasty little twinks there up for a kiss and a cuddle. It helps that Coach Drevin is out and proud, so the Panthers has a rep for attracting gay guys to the team. Yeah, this town is kinda run down, but it's also got a few sweet things goin' for it, too.

I jostle my dick in my shorts as the trolley approaches. Like everything around here, all the cars on the line are rickety and basically held together with hope and a prayer. I didn't believe there even were streetcars until I got here. I thought they only existed in San Francisco or whatever. But that's just another weird quirk of this place.

Even though the paint is peeling and sometimes you feel like they're gonna rattle off the damn rails, I think they have a kinda charm about them. They get you where you gotta go in any case, and are way cheaper than an Uber. Handy for times like now where I don't wanna go get my old rust bucket from the stadium parking lot because I fully intend on drinking as many beers as it takes to make me forget that I apparently own Logan McKenna a whole friggin' grand.

"Evenin', ma'am," I say to my favorite driver, Effie. She has an amazing afro hairstyle that takes up most of the space in her cab. She also ain't afraid to talk shit at me.

"Heard you boys got your asses handed to you," she quips as I drop my coins in the ticket machine.

"Yeah, yeah," I say good-naturedly and wink at her. "You just keep thinkin' bout my ass, ma'am."

She snorts and waves me along, her blood-red nails long and pointy, like she's just killed a man for less. "You sit that ass down now so I can take these fine folks where they need to go."

I know where I need to go. My junk is already getting a bit chubby at the thought of someone tasty to play with. Mercifully, no one can see that as I sit down on the trolley. But yeah, I think that's what I need. A good dance, and maybe a good fuck if I'm lucky. That'll push all the Not Allowed thoughts out of my brain about Gabe and Seth.

I have a bad habit of falling in love with every gorgeous guy I meet, I'm aware. I'm not great at dating, though. Dudes always want me to, like, take charge because I'm usually the bigger one. But that's not my jam. I'm easy when it comes to topping or bottoming. In fact, I'd like to bottom a lot more than I usually do. I like a guy who will boss me around, y'know? But because of my size, I don't ever seem to attract guys like that.

Oh, well. Maybe I'll find myself a feisty little brat tonight. That could be fun. Even if we don't have sex, I'd really like to just kiss someone. Kissing is amazing. I love it. And I give the best hugs.

Maybe not when I do them at full speed, as Seth pointed out. Oops. He did kind of have a point there.

At least I've got a chance to make it up to him now! Gabe

is going to help him fix his credits situation, and I'll be super serious, like he wants. I won't goof around, so he can study his ass off. Then he'll get to play for the scouts like he planned. Not that awful guy Perkins who only cares about himself and not the team at all. I think Seth really does have what it takes to go pro. Man, I'd be so proud of him.

And if I can get my diploma as well, that'll be the cherry on top.

Grinning, I get my phone back out of my pocket and make a new group with Gabe's number. I've got Seth's already from our team chat, so it's easy to put the three of us in touch. I call it 'Study Buddies' and make the icon a photo of a bright red apple. I'm not sure what apples have to do with being smart, but it looks cool, so I don't worry about it. Hey! Maybe Gabe will know. He seems like he would.

"Hey, Gabe!" I mumble out loud to myself as I type out the first message between us. "Me and Seth are ALL IN and will be at the library tomorrow at ten o'clock like you said. We'll make sure we have pens and paper and all that stuff! Thanks, bro. You're the best. I'll bring snacks to keep us energized! Sleep tight."

I add a bunch of emojis and hit send. You've got to admit that giving up your Sunday morning for two dudes you don't know out of the goodness of your heart is a pretty rad thing to do. I'm looking forward to getting to know this little freshman a whole lot better.

I look out the window as the familiar route takes me into the center of town. If you pay attention, you can see just how many places got the McKenna name on them these days. Even since I came here, I can see the difference. That Logan guy really thinks he owns everything.

Well, he doesn't own me nor Seth. Nor little Gabe Visoth. We're a team now, and maybe there's a cat's chance in hell I might graduate after all.

That's a tomorrow problem, though. Tonight, I'm going to have fun and let off all my steam. Because tomorrow I'm going to be a thousand percent serious and not think about how hot Gabe is or how much I want Seth to be my friend. My mind is going to be totally focused on books and facts and all that smart stuff.

No shenanigans allowed.

# CHAPTER 4
## *Gabe*

I'M A NERVOUS WRECK AS I SIT AT ONE OF THE LIBRARY TABLES, checking my watch every ten seconds. It's five after now, and I'm resisting the urge to message the new group chat, asking if they're still coming. But I'm too afraid.

It would make sense if they stood me up. They're about a million times cooler than I am and would probably rather do anything else than hang out with me here on their weekend.

"Athena, grant me patience," I mumble, tapping my nose with the end of my pen.

I've been talking a lot to the Greek goddess of wisdom since last night, mostly asking her what on earth I'm doing. Have I lost my mind? I've always been fascinated by the ancient Greek gods, but I never started talking to them until I left home for college.

It's not the same as talking to the real god like Mama does at church, I know. I hope I'm not being sacrilegious. But I get more comfort from talking to the likes of Zeus, Ares, Artemis, and Dionysus, probably because I *don't* believe they're real. Plus, I like that I can talk to different gods about different, specific things.

I've been interested in studying classics for years. That's why I came to Paddle Creek College. It's not exactly a renowned institution. Its main attraction is the gay-friendly football team, which was certainly an added bonus for me. That's what draws students from out of state, usually. The rest are typically locals.

However, their newest classics professor changed all that, at least for me. Benedict Knight used to teach at Oxford University in England before coming here of all places for whatever reason. But when I saw his credentials, I knew this was where I had to come despite my parents' protests that it was too far away. They don't think I need a degree anyway, especially Mama. But Professor Knight is a genius, and learning from him has already been such a privilege.

Gods, listen to me. I'm such a nerd. No wonder Seth and Marty have stood me up.

I can't change who I am, though, as evidenced by why the library is my favorite place to be, even on a Sunday morning. I have to admit that it's where I feel most centered in the whole college. I love the smell of the books and the quiet calm. My roommate doesn't seem to be aware of the invention of headphones, and is always blasting music every waking hour. This is my sanctuary.

But my usual sense of harmony is eluding me as I check my watch again. I shouldn't be as disappointed as I am. This wasn't a *date*, after all. Not that I've ever been on one of those. Definitely not with both guys at the same time—that would be crazy. If they never speak to me again, I'll just be grateful they ever interacted with me at all. I feel like I've met my favorite celebrities, and it would be greedy to expect more.

Except my heart leaps when the door suddenly swings open to reveal both Seth and Marty walking in together. Marty's taller, so he holds the door for Seth to walk through, a grin on his happy face. Seth is chewing his lip and frowning slightly, which worries me. But he's here, and that's all that really matters.

Before I can stop myself, I wave excitedly at them like a total dork. I snatch my hand back down when I realize what I've done, but then Marty is waving back with just as much enthusiasm, and I don't feel quite so stupid.

They make their way past several other tables toward the corner I nabbed for us near the stacks. It's normally pretty quiet in this area, I think because it's also near the fire escape, but it's not like anyone actually uses that door, so it's my favorite spot.

"Hi," I say breathlessly as I stand up to greet them. "You came."

*Duh.* Of course they did. They're standing right there. Smooth, Gabe, smooth.

"Hey, little dude," Marty says enthusiastically. "Yeah, totally. I waited outside for a bit to meet this one, though, so we could come in together. I figured you'd be cool chilling here cuz it's, like, your place."

He looks around as if he's never stepped foot in this building before, which...I mean, he's a lovely guy, but I wouldn't be surprised if that were the case.

Plus...wowzers. That's not the first term of endearment he's called me. One of the Paddle Creek frigging Panthers has nicknames for me. And he's thought about me enough to realize that I'd be content chilling in the library? That's pretty cool. I would have thought he'd have forgotten me the moment I walked away from him last night.

It takes me a second to recover and remember how words work. "Oh, yeah, I love it here," I admit. "I'm glad you came. Everything was kind of crazy last night, but I really believe this is going to work."

Seth pulls out the chair opposite me on the rectangular

table to take a seat. I drop back down where I've been waiting and am then not surprised when Marty whips the chair around and sits on it backward. He drops his backpack to the floor then pulls out a pen and a pad of paper.

That's it.

At least Seth retrieves a stack of course books from his own bag and a ring binder of notes as well as his notepad. But then he fixes me with an intense stare.

"I feel like we got off to a chaotic start last night," he says, and I lick my lips, feeling anxious. Is he going to tell me off for getting involved?

"Yeah," I say with a weak chuckle. "But…it could all be for the best. I truly believe I can help you." I look at Marty. "Help you both." I want to make that clear. I know Seth has a *lot* riding on this success, but I'm not abandoning Marty.

Seth rubs his lower lip. "Do you want us to tell people about this? Because I'd rather keep my fragile grades situation to myself for now."

Oh gods.

He thinks I'm doing this to get *popular?*

That's so ridiculous I burst out laughing. I quickly clap my hand over my mouth and glance toward the librarian's desk, but thankfully, right now it's empty. Good. She's a bit scary.

"Oh, you don't have to tell a soul," I say, almost giddy. That's the absolute farthest thing from my mind.

"So…you're really just being nice?" he asks, like that's so unusual. I get it. He's a rock star in this town. He must have people trying to use and manipulate him all the time.

I decide to come clean.

"I've already explained that I really love learning this arts stuff," I say as I pick up a pen and start doodling more squiggles in the margin of my open notebook to distract myself.

"And I don't like bullies. Logan was being awful to you guys. And, well, um…"

I inhale and then swallow, my eyes still focused on my doodle.

"There was this game a couple of weeks ago," I begin to explain. "One of our guys"— I purposefully don't name him, as that doesn't seem classy —"speared a player on the opposing team and really hurt him. Like I think he broke his leg or something."

"Fucking Perkins," Seth snarls, clearly remembering the incident I'm recalling. I'm not sure why, but it warms my heart that he's still outraged by it.

"Anyway," I wave my hand because that detail doesn't matter for the sake of this story. "Marty, you ran to him and held his hand until the medical staff got to him, not caring all his teammates were screaming at you. And, Seth, *you* screamed at the guy—Perkins—for playing dangerously. You, um, really didn't have to do that. No one would have blamed you for taking that time to hustle your own team to take advantage of the break in the game. But you played fair. I just really, really admired that."

Marty blinks, then looks at Seth, who equally looks stunned. "You were there?" Seth asks me.

"You *remember* that?" Marty chimes in. *"I* barely remember that."

I nod and swirl my pen over the paper some more, looking down where it's safer. "You both behaved like gentlemen. It, um, struck a chord with me."

There's a beat. "That's a good thing, right?" Marty asks.

I can't help but laugh. I think it's from relief. "Yeah," I say warmly. "Really good. So that's why I'm helping you guys, Seth. Because you already showed me that you're prepared to help others, even when there's nothing in it for you. Just because it's the right thing to do."

Seth stares at me for a few moments with his astonishingly beautiful green eyes. *Jeepers.* He's like a god of old, and I'm a mere mortal. He shouldn't be looking at me like that. It goes against the laws of nature.

"Okay, then," he mutters before flipping open his ring binder and riffling through the sheets. "I think this might work, after all. But let's maybe try some actual work first. I've got a philosophy paper due on this cave thing that I have no fucking clue about. If you can talk me" —he arches an eyebrow at Marty— "*us* through it so we can write half-decent papers, perhaps this thing will work."

I feel myself light up from within. "Plato's Allegory of the Cave?" I prompt. He checks his notes with a frown, then nods. I try and repress a squeal. *See,* I knew I would be able to handle senior year work. "I can absolutely talk you through that. It's wildly fascinating. Don't worry. I know you'll get it right away once we pull it apart. It's all about perspective."

"Aww, little dude," Marty says fondly. "You really do love this shit, don't you?"

I try not to blush, but it doesn't work. "Yeah. It makes me feel connected to something that's thousands of years old but still so relevant today," I say softly.

Marty nods sagely. "Rad," he says.

"It is radical," I agree.

I think of my frighteningly Christian upbringing and what my mother would say if she knew the true extent of my studies these days.

Then I grin broader.

"Shall we get started?"

# CHAPTER 5

*Seth*

THE NEXT FEW WEEKS FLY BY. I WON'T LIE—I'M FUCKING exhausted. Between games, practice, going to every single one of my classes, and extra study sessions with Gabe, I barely get time to breathe let alone sleep.

But...I'm also kind of happy and content in a way I've never experienced before. It's weird. Classes were always something I had to endure. Back in Chicago, I did okay through high school, but that was mostly because I had an amazing guidance counselor. Between her and my mom, they always managed to check up on what I was doing and remind me if coursework was due or I had an exam coming up, that kind of thing.

It started out okay when I got to college, but obviously things have fallen apart by the time I got to my final year because I've been so damned obsessed with the team and going pro. I'm ashamed that I just *forgot* what classes I was supposed to be taking and how many credits I needed from each course to get enough to graduate.

But Gabe knows.

That little cutie seems to know *everything.*

He's drawn up a plan to get me through all the work I have to make up and worked out what tests I need to ask my professors to take or retake to up my GPA for the semester. We're focusing most on the classics department. I don't really mind. I feel about as indifferent to everything that isn't football.

But it made sense because one, it's Gabe's favorite subject and two, the senior professor is a guy named Knight, who's not a dick at all. He's firm but fair, and was sympathetic when I explained how hard I'm working to make up everything. He even offered me some one-on-one sessions himself, as well as independent studies for next semester to hit my credit hours, and I've realized that I'm now kind of enjoying his classes these days.

I'm enjoying most of my classes more than I used to, actually. It's amazing what a difference it makes that I'm not struggling so badly anymore. Now that I understand so much more of what's being discussed in every lesson, it feels like a glass wall has come down between me and the books. I always thought I was kind of dumb, but it turns out that I'm pretty smart when I apply myself.

And it's all thanks to Gabe.

He's working wonders with Quinn as well. He has less to make up, as technically he's done all his credits. Whether he did them well is another story, but they're not worrying about that. Gabe is drilling him to retake the tests he failed before, then focusing super hard on preparing Quinn for the end-of-semester exams.

We've practically set up camp at that corner table in the library. I noticed that after the first week, a little 'reserved' sign had appeared. I remember being disappointed that someone had taken our special spot. But when I asked the scary librarian, Ms. Maude, what time the other people needed it, she just peered over her bejeweled horn-rimmed glasses and said it was for us. The *obviously* wasn't spoken aloud, but it was heavily implied.

Since I'm pretty certain Ms. Maude is secretly a real live witch, I just thanked her and scuttled away again.

So that's where we are on a Friday afternoon. Usually, when we don't have a game, we take the weekend to blow off steam, but today there's nowhere I'd rather be than with little Gabe Visoth, going over Latin verb tables.

He's helped me understand that studying philosophy is kind of like practicing plays for the team, and verb structures are like lifting weights at the gym. But instead of working out my body, I'm working out my brain. It all seemed a lot cooler after that sank in.

This is one of the lessons we can do with Quinn as well. I have to admit I'm fucking stunned that he's kept his promise. He hasn't skipped one of our sessions so far, and he's done all the assignments that Gabe has given him, even if sometimes he misses the mark and Gabe has to go through it all again with him. I used to find Quinn's perpetual positivity grating. But it turns out that when he's putting it toward a good cause, it's actually kind of endearing.

And I really *would* be a dumbass to miss how stunningly hot he is. I've seen him naked many times in the locker room, so I also know that he's a big boy *everywhere.* Not that I'm interested in bottoming. But I'd be lying if I hadn't thought a lot more about sucking that beast these past few weeks.

I've never really had a boyfriend before. I like playing the field (obviously) and have never struggled to find a cute ass to smash whenever I felt like it. So I've always gone for looks and not cared much about personality.

It's true that Gabe did it for me the second I laid eyes on him. He's got this blond curly hair like a frigging angel that sits around his ears—enough to get a really good handful of.

His skin is a warm tan, and his eyes are a sparkling blue, like the ocean.

But it's little things that are getting to me, like the way he doodles all over his notebooks, even when he's talking or reading, like he's got two sides of his brain working at once, concentrating on different things. He's got endless patience for me and Quinn, even when I know we're being meatheads and he has to explain things several times before we get them.

Then there's his massive kind heart, and I'm not just talking about what he's doing for me and Quinn.

When we came out of the library particularly late one night, we disturbed Clayton, the campus's local trash panda, riffling through a nearby garbage can. At first, Gabe had been shocked, jumping back against me. It took everything I had not to wrap my arms around him to protect him, but instead, I gave him a squeeze and let him go, explaining that Clayton is kind of an institution around here. Like a mascot. The grumpy janitor likes to chase him off with a broom, but I know Ms. Maude leaves whole frigging sandwiches out for the little guy.

The next time we left the library, I totally caught my nerd dumping an entire bag of trail mix behind the bushes.

But I'm getting to understand that's just who he is. He doesn't see a pest. He sees a hungry buddy in need of help. Just like he didn't see two dumb jocks who deserved to fail when he came to our rescue from that douche McKenna.

It's getting more difficult not to think about his sweet face whenever I finally do fall into bed every night. I haven't even felt like going out and getting laid since we started our tutoring sessions. At first, I just jerked off to porn with blond twinks in them, telling myself that was okay. But then it became harder and harder not to just close my eyes and think of his beautiful face and delicate, tinkling laugh.

But I have to stop. I can't think of him like that, at least not right now. He's so fucking innocent, and he's doing me the favor of a lifetime.

But there's another problem, too.

I've noticed Quinn also looking at him with cartoon love hearts in his eyes. In those moments, it doesn't matter that our team rivalry seems to have quieted down. I appreciate that the stupid pranks have stopped and how hard he's working on his studies.

But if it comes down to a bro-down between us for Gabe's affection, I don't care that he's bigger than me.

I'll win.

I've been toying with the idea that after I graduate, I should have some time before I move to be with whatever team signs me (if I get signed, Jesus fucking Christ). Maybe *then* I could take Gabe out—actually go on some proper dates for once. It's not like I need to get to know him. That's happened naturally already.

But I figure he deserves some romancing before I blow his mind with the best sex of his life.

I realize I'm lost in thought and chewing the end of my pen as he explains something about third conjugations. His lips are pink and plump. God, they'd look amazing stretched over my cock. His nose is like a button, and his skin is a little flushed around his collar as it always is when he gets excited about some dorky thing, like Latin verbs.

But am I the bigger dork because I think that's fucking adorable? Or a massive slut because I just want to see how red I can make him all the time?

His phone screen lights up, yanking his attention away midsentence. It's on silent with no vibration seeing as we're in the library. The caller ID reads 'Mom,' and I expect him to smile or look happy or something. My mom only bothers me a couple of times a month because she knows what my schedule is like, but I always appreciate hearing her voice and finding out what crazy DIY project my old man has started this time.

I'm surprised when his eyes go wide. He almost looks panicky. For a second, he just stares at the glowing screen before his hand shoots out, and he hits the red reject button, sending it to voicemail.

"S-sorry about that," he stutters.

I frown. "We can take a break if you want to call your mom back," I say.

He shakes his head. "No, it's fine. I—"

The screen lights up again.

This time he gulps and cuts the call immediately. He's biting his lip and practically trembling. "Sorry," he whispers once more.

My frown deepens. Come to think of it, I can't remember him ever mentioning his mom or his family before. Maybe they're not close? But...I *have* seen him on his phone a lot. Often as he's walking up to the library when he hastily closes the call.

"You don't need to be sorry, little man," Quinn says, unusually serious for him. "But what if it's an emergency?"

"No, it's not. I—"

He's interrupted as a text message pops up.

*Are you ghosting me, young man?* it reads from his mother.

"I talked to her this morning," he mumbles miserably.

Something raw and angry is clawing at my chest. I am not okay with anything that takes the pretty smile off my boy's face, even if it is his own mother. But before I can open my mouth, he's standing from his chair.

"I'm so sorry," he says for the third time as he clutches his cell to his chest. "I really should call her back. Will you be all right without me for a few minutes?"

"Of course, bro," Quinn says sincerely. "Take all the time you need."

I manage to wrestle with myself until Gabe steps outside the library door, but then I lose the fight.

"Nope," I say, more to myself than Quinn, before striding out after our little tutor into the courtyard.

There are people milling around, but he's walking around the building to a secluded spot with a stone bench and all kinds of pretty trailing autumn flowers and bushes. The only kind I recognize are roses in several different shades, but the overall effect is damned beautiful, especially with the fall colors on the trees. I never even knew this was here. It's cute, like he is.

Right now, he still might be cute, but he's also clearly distraught. He turns to face me, the phone already to his ear. He looks horrified when he realizes I've followed him, but unfortunately, a kind of caveman has overcome me, and the urge to protect him is stronger than anything else.

"It's okay," I tell him, not sure how he'll react to that. If he tells me to fuck off, I'll try and respect that. He might need privacy. But everything inside me is screaming that I need to stay.

Luckily, he sags in relief and nods. Good. I didn't want to fight him on this because he needs me, whether he knows it or not.

It's quiet enough that I can hear the dialing tone down the line. I gesture for him to sit on the bench, then I join him and rest my hand on his shoulder. I can tell he's spooked, so of course I'm going to sit here and take care of him. I'd do it for any of the guys on my team.

I probably wouldn't be rubbing my thumb in soothing circles over their collarbone, but whatever.

"Mom?" he cries suddenly.

"Where have you been?" I'm just about able to make out faintly. "I kept getting your voicemail."

He swallows, and I can feel him trembling. "I-I'm sorry. I must be in a bad signal area."

My eyebrows raise at the lie. Not that he told it. I think a white lie to save face is fine every now and again. It's more the fact that he had to tell it at all. She's really this mad because he didn't drop everything to talk to her? He said they spoke this morning, for fuck's sake.

"You've got excellent coverage across the entire campus. I've checked," she snips back. Whoa, lady. Stalker much? "Are you off gallivanting with a girl somewhere?"

Gabe splutters, and I can't blame him. That's a pretty big fucking leap for her to make. And 'girl'? Is this lady serious? It's really obvious that Gabe is gay. Well, I think so, anyway.

"Mama! No!" he practically shrieks. "Of course not. I promised you and Tata, remember? No dating until after college."

Again, what the fuck? Why should she have any say in his dating life?

"Then why have you been avoiding me these past few weeks? Honestly, Gabriel. I think you're becoming very selfish. I think maybe you should move back home and give up on this nonsense."

"W-what?" he gasps. "No! I mean—I'm so sorry. I've just been studying like crazy this semester, as we'll have all our final papers and tests soon. I'm not avoiding you. I swear!"

She hums, but it's more like a growl. I can feel my other fist curling into a tight ball. But I make sure to keep up the soothing little circles with my other thumb, trying to anchor my boy as this woman loses her mind at him on the other end of the call.

Seriously? He misses a few phone calls, and she wants to

come and drag him back to her house? That sounds kind of psycho to me.

Quinn appears. For a second, I want to tell him to fuck off. *I'm* looking after Gabe, and I don't need backup. But then he takes one look at Gabe's crumbling, distressed face and drops to the ground in front of Gabe, placing his huge hands on his knees and looking up at him with such big puppy dog eyes that something stutters in my chest.

Actually, you know what? Gabe is so upset right now that I want him to have all the support he can get. If that's from both me and Quinn, maybe that's not such a bad thing. In fact, something tiny blossoms in my chest that feels like gratitude toward my teammate.

Gabe deserves the best of everything.

I realize I've tuned out and missed what Gabe's mom has been saying. "I promise I'll pick up the phone whenever I can," he's telling her. "I know it's rude and ungrateful. I'm so sorry. I never meant to disrespect you. I just want to make you and Tata proud, I swear."

"You'd make him prouder here at the restaurant. You know he's depending on you to take over once he retires. I don't know how going to college is going to teach you anything he can't."

My eyebrows shoot up, and I share a look with Quinn. Our shy little philosopher running a busy restaurant? He'd hate that. I know I've only known him a few weeks, but of that, I'm sure. He's a thinker. A dreamer. His brain is like that chocolate factory in that kid's book. All wild and colorful.

"I got the scholarship," he whispers. It sounds like a pitiful argument. Like he knows that, ultimately, he's just delaying the inevitable.

"Yeah, yeah," she says with a laugh. "You're right. Tata and I said we'd let you go see the world a little before you came home. I'm sorry. I'm just so tired. I worry when you don't pick up."

"I know," he replies guiltily. "I'll keep a better eye on my phone. I don't want to worry you guys."

"I know, chico. You're a good boy."

"Thank you," he says, but he sounds defeated. Then he looks around and seems to realize that Quinn and I are there with him, and the color drains from his face. "My, um, study group is waiting for me, though. I better get back to them."

His mother sighs. "Okay, Gabriel. Call me tomorrow, please."

"I will. I promise," he tells her eagerly.

They say their goodbyes, and he finally hangs up the phone.

Then he looks at me in fear.

I am not fucking having that.

# CHAPTER 6

## *Gabe*

HOLY SMOKES, SETH LOOKS PISSED. I THINK I'M GOING TO BE sick.

"I-I'm so sorry I ran out on studying," I manage to utter. "We can go back right now. I'll stay later if you're able to. I understand if you have plans, though. I can meet you earlier tomorrow. I can make up the time. I—"

"Whoa, whoa, slow down, bubbelah," he says. His voice has a warmth and concern to it that I've never heard before. The hand that's been holding my shoulder moves up to cup the back of my neck, and my heart stutters. He's staring intently at me with his green eyes. "I don't care about a few minutes missed on Latin verbs. I care that you're upset."

I gulp. I can feel my eyes are damp as I look from him to Marty, who nods at me in support. "Totally, bro," he says sincerely. "We're a team now. Me and Seth here don't want you sad, not if we can help it."

My mouth opens and closes a couple of times. "It's my own fault," I finally manage to whisper. "I *have* been avoiding her. But she calls all the time. Sometimes three or four times a day. I just…I want to have some time to myself. That's what college is supposed to be about, right?"

"It is," Seth says firmly. "It's about finding out who you really are. And you shouldn't feel guilty or anything. That's a *lot* of times to be calling a day."

"It sounds like she's having trouble letting go of her little bird," Marty says kindly.

I nod. That's so true. But I also know that it's been hard for her, and I'm being a bad son. I feel terrible that I've been trying to put a bit of distance between us, but sometimes it's like she's trying to smother me.

I take a few breaths. Growing up, I often felt like my mom was my whole life and there was nothing worse than her disapproval. But then I look between Seth and Marty as they watch me with such concern, and I realize that there might not be any *better* feeling than that.

They care about me.

It's crazy, and maybe I'm imagining things, but it feels like we're actually becoming friends. I've been so focused on studying and keeping my nose clean that I can't really say that I've made any actual friends here in Paddle Creek. I never had any deep relationships in high school, either. I've always been too afraid that people would reject me, so I stayed away. But it was horribly lonely at times.

It's different with Seth and Marty. We don't just discuss studying in our little chat group now. Marty will always send photos when he spies Clayton, the campus raccoon, which makes me smile. Seth likes to remind me to eat because sometimes I do forget. He'll send photos of his protein shakes or of all the yummy-looking things he eats on his cheat days. We talk about our professors and stuff we've seen on TV or cool TikToks. Shoot, we even talk about the *weather.*

I feel like they're in my pocket every day with me, even

when we're not studying. I know I'm going to miss them when they're gone. But I'm trying to enjoy the unbelievable experience while it lasts.

I worried for a second it was going to all be over just now. I genuinely thought Seth was mad at me for abandoning them for my mom, but he's still rubbing the back of my neck and looking at me like he's really concerned.

I take a shaky breath and manage a small smile. "I think I'm okay now, thank you. We should go back and study."

Marty blows a raspberry from where he's still kneeling at my feet. His hands are heavy on my legs, but in a nice way. Like my weighted blanket that helps so much with my anxiety. He looks at Seth.

"I know I said I wouldn't goof off, but I think we all deserve a break. We've worked our asses off for weeks now, and it's a Friday night with no game for once. Why don't we thank our little genius here by taking him down to Creams?"

I raise my eyebrows. I don't know what that means, but is he seriously suggesting the two of them spend time with me outside of the library?

Seth exhales and gives us a rare, beaming smile. "You know what? That sounds like an awesome plan. What do you say, Gabe? Have you ever been to the Ice Cream Parlor?"

I try not to blush. "Um, no. Do they do sundaes?"

They both laugh, but it's really not unkind. In fact, they both rub their thumbs against my neck and legs affectionately.

"It's the best gay bar in the whole of northern Indiana," Seth says kindly, like he's really not judging me for not knowing. But then he raises his eyebrows and flicks his gaze briefly toward my phone, which is still clutched between my hands. "Oh, unless that's not your thing. Your mom said something about a girlfriend?"

I groan. I had a feeling he could hear her side of the

conversation as well. "No, um, no," I say, shaking my head. "I definitely don't have a girlfriend. I…that bar sounds fun."

I chicken out of admitting out loud that I'm gay. I haven't said that to *anyone* yet. I know by saying I want to go there, it's sort of the same thing. I certainly haven't denied being gay since I got here. I even quietly joined the LGBT alliance during orientation. I've never been on a date, though, or kissed a guy, let alone…*you-know-what.*

But it seems so monumental to finally come clean that I can't do it right now when I'm unprepared.

I know my mom will hate it if she ever found out. My dad will almost certainly never speak to me again. They'll say I'm bringing shame down upon them. So I was really hoping to maybe find the freedom to be myself here in Paddle Creek and keep it separate from my home life in Missouri.

The Ice Cream Parlor sounds incredibly exciting. My heart is already pounding at the thought of going. It seems like I really have been sheltering myself under my studies if I've never heard of it until now, but that doesn't really matter.

Not when Seth Eisen and Marty Quinn are offering to take me.

I thought it was astonishing when I first got here that they were out and proud football players on the team. They aren't even the only ones. It's like the opposite of New Belleville—the small town where I grew up—where anyone who dares to be different in any way is scorned and ostracized.

"Are you sure?" Seth asks. "They'd stamp you so you can't drink because you're underage, but it's still a cool place to dance and stuff. Or we could do something else, anything you want."

I bite my lip, my heart fluttering in my chest. He's really

tying himself up in knots to find a way to make me feel better. It's like I'm in some kind of dream.

"The bar sounds good," I say with as much confidence as I can muster. "Letting off some steam sounds fun." I lick my lips as I look between them. I hate that I have to ask, but I do. "I don't mind if you want to go with other friends, though. You don't have to be seen with me."

They both blink at me. Marty is the first to break the long pause by bursting out laughing. "Why would we *ditch* you, darlin'? We literally just invited you." He slaps my knee. As usual, he doesn't know his own strength and it's a bit hard, but I don't mind. I like that he feels familiar enough with me to do it. "The whole point is to hang out together. Right, Seth?"

I glance over at Seth, who nods sincerely. His fingers are *still* caressing the back of my neck, and it's doing all sorts of strange things to my body. My tummy is all fluttery, and my *you-know-what* is aching between my legs.

"I said I didn't want the whole world to know I was failing my classes," he says eventually, his words warm like melting butter. "I never said that I didn't want to be seen with you, bubbelah. That was just your interpretation." His grin is lopsided to let me know that he's gently teasing me.

"I do love to overthink things," I agree.

That's the second time he's called me 'bubbelah' this evening. I'm pretty sure it means sweetie or something like that.

Seth Eisen is calling me sweetheart. Marty Quinn is calling me darling.

It's like I've stepped into a parallel universe. One I don't want to leave.

"Okay," I say, puffing out my cheeks. "Shall we go get our bags? We left everything in the library."

Marty laughs as he stands, and offers me his hand to help

me up as well. "Don't worry. Ms. Maude would curse anyone who messed with our stuff, I'm sure."

"I thought she was a witch, too!" Seth cries as he also gets up. "She's got all those crystals all over the check-out desk."

"There's a black cat that sleeps in her office," I say, thrilled that I have a little tidbit that makes them both raise their eyebrows.

"Definitely a witch," Marty says in awe.

"But if she's on our side, that makes her a good witch," Seth says like he's imparting profound knowledge.

I giggle, slipping my phone into my pocket and finally letting that horrible conversation go. I'm going to forget about my mom stressing me out, and I'm going to go hang out with my new friends, who happen to be two of the coolest guys in all of Paddle Creek College at an actual gay bar.

How is this my life?

# CHAPTER 7
## *Gabe*

WE'VE ALL GOT OUR BAGS WITH US AT THE LIBRARY STILL, SO Seth insists that we each go home, drop off our stuff, then he says that he and Marty would pick me up in an Uber as they want to drink so that rules out driving. That seems a little extravagant to me when we could just take the trolley, but Seth has this way of insisting on things, so I let it go and accept the nice gesture.

If I'm going to my very first gay bar, I want to look and feel good. Mercifully, my obnoxious roommate is already out for the evening, so I have space to rush through a shower and then frantically try and find an outfit I like. I'm so nervous. I don't want to embarrass the guys, even after what they said and how nice they were to me out in the courtyard. If they see any of their teammates, I don't want anyone to wonder what the hell some dork is doing hanging out with Paddle Creek's star players.

I take the time to put contact lenses in so I'm not wearing my glasses for once, then hurry to find my nicest pair of jeans. I wipe down my sneakers so they're not so scuffed, then I stand in front of the mirror for what feels like ages trying to decide on a T-shirt or a button-down or what. When my phone lights up with a message in the group chat to say they're outside in the car, I hastily throw on a tight tee with a cute dragon on as well as an open gray shirt over the top.

There. Kind of cool, or at least I hope so.

I remember just in time to spritz some aftershave on before I grab my keys, wallet, and phone, then hurtle down the stairs. Before I open the door leading out of my dorm, I stop and take a deep breath to compose myself, saying a quick thanks to Aphrodite, even if this *definitely* isn't a date. But my heart is certainly fluttering, so I pray to her anyway.

Please don't let me embarrass myself.

Then I walk out to see the waiting Uber.

"Hey!" Marty cries, hopping out and waving to me. "Aw, you look great, little dude."

I blush. "T-thanks," I stutter. "You, too."

That's an understatement. He's wearing a top that looks practically sprayed on, made of a fine, slippery-looking material that clings to his immense body.

I slide into the backseat and realize Seth's sitting there as well, not in the front like I assumed. He's wearing a purple silk shirt with the top few buttons undone so I can see his collarbones.

Aaaand then Marty gets in next to me, and I'm suddenly sandwiched between their muscular thighs.

I freeze. I can barely breathe. Oh, gods. What's happening?

"Here," Seth says warmly, offering me the middle seat belt. I just sort of stare at it for a second, my brain not working properly. But before it can get weird, Marty grabs the buckle and secures it between us.

Cuz that's not weird at all.

"There we go. All good, sir," Marty tells the driver cheerfully.

I gulp, my faculties sort of coming back to me. "Thanks," I say again, this time without stuttering. Damn, I'm nervous.

"No problem," they both say at the same time.

It's funny. That super strong rivalry they had seems to be melting away more each day. First, they fought over who I'd tutor. Now they're working together to do something so simple as secure my belt. I should feel embarrassed that my body failed to manage to even make my arms work. However, seeing them acting like a team for *me* is worth it.

They spend the short drive chatting easily about a team they're going to be playing soon, and their voices soothe me, helping me to relax a little. By the time the car stops, I'm not trembling, at least.

We're on a street more toward the quieter end of Paddle Creek. I've never been to this part of the small town before, so it's not so surprising that I wasn't aware of the bar until now. Because, to be honest, there's absolutely *no* missing it. The sign is made out of bright red neon lights in a vintage font, and there's a giant ice cream cone sculpture by the door. There's also a rainbow flag fluttering from a pole hanging overhead that makes my heart ache. Just seeing such a basic sign that these are my people makes me feel almost weak at the knees.

As I step out of the car toward the bar, confidence and daring rush through me. If I'd have known a year ago that I'd be going to an actual gay bar out in the open where anyone could see me, I'd have never believed it. My audacity makes me giddy, especially after Seth pays the driver and he and Marty come to join me. I'm not only going to a gay bar. I'm going with two *insanely* hot guys.

Wow.

"Are you ready?" Seth asks.

I lick my lips and look at the people hanging around outside. It's mostly guys but there are also some women and people who probably identify as something in between. These *are* my people.

I'm so ready.

"Yes," I say with a grin, and they lead me inside.

The walls are a beautiful minty green color, whereas the booths and stools at the bar are finished with red leather. There's a jukebox and a special booth that's made out of a real Cadillac finished in green, just like the walls. It looks like a VIP area, and the people there are sharing a giant cocktail bowl with ice cream floating on the top, each with an extra-large straw to drink from.

There aren't that many people on the dance floor yet, so I can see it's made of large black-and-white-checkered tiles. There are neon lights everywhere, and the sound system is pumping a contemporary pop track, but not so loud that I can't hear Seth when he leans in and asks what I'd like to drink.

"Oh, um, I don't know," I say, looking around as if I might spy what other people are having and be able to make a decision quickly enough. But aside from the giant Coke float, it's hard to tell in the dark. "What are you having?"

Seth raises his eyebrows at Marty. "Beer?"

"Sure, bro!" Marty agrees excitedly.

"What would you like?" Seth asks me.

I haven't drunk much alcohol in my life, but in that moment I kind of wish I was old enough to so that I wasn't the odd one out. What do people drink in nightclubs?

Seth clicks his fingers. "I know. How about a virgin strawberry daiquiri? It's like a slushie."

I try not to blush at the V-word. Obviously he doesn't mean it like that, but in that moment, I feel like I've got a neon sign flashing over my head announcing that I've never even kissed a guy before.

"They have other flavors as well," Marty chimes in, pointing to the bar. Seth was right. They do have slushie machines set up, but these don't look like they're for kids. There's pineapple and mango as well, and they have versions mixed with alcohol as well as alcohol free.

I love that they're fretting over my drinks order. This is crazy.

"Strawberry sounds great," I say with an excited smile. "Thank you."

Seth juts his chin at Marty. "Do you guys want to try and grab a table? I'll get this round."

"Hell, yeah!" Marty says with a thumbs-up.

Then he places his hand *on my lower back* and starts gently guiding me around to look and see if we can find some-where. My feet basically work on autopilot because my brain is entirely preoccupied with where he's touching me.

Also, Seth paid for the Uber, and now he's getting the drinks? It's too much. But it doesn't seem like I have much choice in the matter—for now, anyway. I worry a lot about money, but the least I can do will be to get a round later.

A group are looking like they might be getting up to leave one of the booths. Marty spots them at the same time as I do, so we pick up the pace and arrive just as the last person is sliding out. A couple of them smile and nod at us, but my attention has already been caught by another group of younger guys who were obviously trying to nab the seats as well.

I'm about to back off and give it to them when the guy leading them does a double take. "Whoa! Marty Quinn!"

I look up to see Marty grin. "Hey, y'all! How's it going?"

His tone is friendly, but not in a way that makes me think that he knows the group. He's just being nice because they know him from the team, and that makes me feel all warm and glowy. Being kind is one of the most important things you can do in life. I think so, anyway.

"G-great," the lead guy says with a big smile. He and his friends are all a bit like me. Kind of smaller and a little fem. For a second, my heart pangs, and I wish that *I* had a gay friendship group like that. Or any friends at all, for that matter. But then I remember that I'm here with Marty frigging Quinn and Seth holy-moly Eisen and decide that my lot could be a lot worse.

"You guys take the table," the guy insists, and his friends nod earnestly. "We're going to be dancing soon, anyway." Then he looks at me—at *me*—and smiles. "Hey, Gabriel."

My mouth drops open. How does he know my name?

Before I can react in any way, Marty rubs my back as he pipes up. "Actually, it's just Gabe. Isn't that right, little dude?"

If possible, my mouth drops even farther. I know that's what I told him and Seth to call me rather than Gabriel, but I hadn't let on why it meant so much to me. I've never explained how I've wanted to be Gabe my whole life, but my mother insisted I remain Gabriel. Otherwise, it would be 'disrespectful' to her and Tata. I couldn't even get away with it at school because she'd give all my teachers strict instructions.

Being Gabe here in Paddle Creek has been liberating, even if it's only really been my teachers using it. I feel like Professor Knight uses it a little more than strictly necessary, possibly because he suspects what it means to me. I might be imagining that. It doesn't mean it doesn't mean everything to me, though.

But to hear Marty actually *correct* these guys makes me feel validated in a way I never thought possible.

"Oh, sure," the guy says as if it's no big deal. "I'm Trystan, by the way. Okay, well, we'll see you in class then, Gabe."

"Y-yeah, sure," I manage to say as they move away.

I turn to look at Marty as he slides into the booth, almost not fitting between the red leather bench and the table because he's so solid. "Um, thanks."

He raises his eyebrows. "For what?"

I fidget on my feet. "For remembering that I like to be called Gabe. It, um, means a lot."

He blinks, then laughs. "Of course, little dude. I remember everything you say." He slaps the seat beside him, making the entire bench bounce. "Come on. Take a load off."

Marty Quinn remembers everything I say?

Somebody pinch me. I must be dreaming.

I do as he asks, and we talk a little bit about the different gay bars he's been to. Apparently, he's been to a lot since he gets to play away with the team so often and always tries to check out new places. I envy his worldliness. My parents didn't believe in vacations other than to our cold and damp cabin thirty miles outside of New Belleville, Missouri. Paddle Creek is the farthest place I've ever been and certainly the most exciting.

I don't admit that to Marty. I just keep asking him questions until Seth arrives with our drinks a few minutes later.

He slides in beside me, and then suddenly, I'm back in another Paddle Creek Panthers sandwich.

This time, I manage not to freeze up completely and even find my voice again after a little while. Having the virgin daiquiri to sip on and distract me probably helps with that. We chat about school but also the Panthers. I think they still don't quite understand that I really love the sport as much as I say I do, but when I start rattling off statistics about their rival teams, they perk up, immediately paying attention. I didn't want to come across like I was trying to impress them or win them over before. But now I'm quite happy to dazzle them. At one point, Seth even gets his phone out and takes some notes.

All of a sudden, the music changes to something with a thumping base and cool guitar riff, and Marty slams his (third, and yes, I did manage to get a round from a passing server) beer bottle down on the table. "Fuck! I *love* this song! Let's dance!"

"Oh, I—" But there's no protesting when Marty's made his mind up. He grabs my hand and practically drags me up. Seth rolls his eyes, downs the last of his beer, then eases his way out of the booth to join us. A gaggle of people quickly nabs our table, so I guess we're committed to dancing now.

I try not to let nerves get the better of me, but I quickly realize that no one's paying any attention to me aside from Marty and Seth. And Marty clearly does love this song as he's thrashing his body about with abandon. It's actually really sweet. He might look large and tough, but he's just a big kid under all that muscle.

I try not to overthink things as I sway my hips and move my arms. But then the song changes again, and Seth has sort of…gravitated closer to me. His hips are moving the same as mine, and he has this easy grin as he dances in front of me. My heart speeds up, and my mouth starts feeling dry. I wish I had some water.

But then he's even closer, looking down at me as we gyrate in time to the beat. I gulp and look him in the eyes. He winks, and I laugh nervously, glancing away. I'm not sure what's happening, but it's like I'm in a spinning top from the loud music, bright lights, and sugary drinks in my system.

He places a hand on my hip.

I gasp and snap my head to look back at him, but we don't stop moving to the music. I know I'm gawking at him, but his smile is lazy and confident. I try and drink some of that energy in to calm me down.

Except then *another* hand slips over my *other* hip, and for the third time that evening, I find myself in a Paddle Creek Panthers sandwich.

But this time it's not just thighs touching.

Marty is pressing his chest to my back. Seth is only technically putting his hand on my hip, but his movements are mirroring mine (or he's encouraging me to mirror him. I can't really tell). His chest is inches from mine, but that also means his *face* is hovering in front of mine. Our noses are practically brushing. It's the almost touching—the possibilities—that is driving me as wild as the physical contact.

Then he closes that gap and bumps our chests together. His breath is ghosting over my lips. Marty's breath flutters over my neck.

What is happening?

No, seriously. What the *fuck* is happening?!

I push at Seth and elbow Marty in his solid gut. Stumbling, I make my way out of the sandwich, my head spinning as I gasp for air. I don't know what I'm doing, let alone saying, but I have to get away. This is too much!

"I'm a *virgin*," I blurt out.

Even in my state, I know there's no coming back from that.

I flee.

# CHAPTER 8

## Seth

I'm man enough to admit when I've fucked up. And, *man*, have I fucked up.

I try and chase after Gabe as he runs through the bar, but an obnoxious bachelorette party all wearing wobbly cocks on headbands, get in my way, trying to grab at me and begging me to dance. "Sorry, no, excuse me," I snap, attempting to be at least a little polite.

"Come on, handsome!" the bride protests. "It's my special night! Just one dance!"

"Aww, sorry, darlin'," Marty drawls from behind me, really turning up the Southern charm. "Maybe next time."

I'm pretty sure she calls us both boring and selfish something or other, but by the time I've pushed through them, I don't care. I'm desperately scanning the bar for my adorable nerd, but he's nowhere to be found.

"Fuck!" I bellow over the music.

Marty squeezes my shoulder. "Let's check outside," he says. I appreciate he knows he fucked up too and is taking this seriously.

We never should have overwhelmed Gabe like that. What was I *thinking?*

I wasn't. That was the problem. Dancing with our little tutor had just felt so damned right in the moment that I hadn't engaged my brain. He's clearly inexperienced—hell—he just yelled at us that he's a virgin, so I know that to be true. But it hadn't felt like we were ganging up on him or pressuring him at all. It had felt like we were protecting him. Enveloping him like a warm embrace.

Until he snapped out of whatever trance-like state he'd been in and fought us off.

"Hey, Dijon," I say to the large dude who greets all the guests at the door. He's even taller in the four-inch heels he's wearing tonight. "Did you see a cute little blond guy come out just now? Maybe in a hurry."

I try not to wince and admit that I'm the reason he would have been hauling ass. Well, *we,* I remind myself as Marty pops up beside me. We did this together.

Dijon grimaces. "I saw a cutie, all right. He hopped on that very trolley." He points to the streetcar disappearing around the corner. "Sorry, sugar."

"Fuck," I say again, balling my fists.

We were supposed to be taking *care* of Gabe tonight after that phone call he got from his mom, not giving him another problem to worry about. Shit, has this ruined everything? I wouldn't blame him if he didn't want to tutor us anymore. Not if he doesn't feel safe.

"Hey, it'll be okay," Marty says as he places a hand on my elbow. "We'll just call him."

I snatch my arm away and scowl. "No, it won't be okay," I bite out. "And don't call him. He needs space. We all do."

With that, I turn on my heels and start the walk home. Maybe some fresh air will clear my head, and I can work out how to un-fuck this situation.

If it can even be un-fucked. Damn, I'm not even thinking about my grades right now. Or the *team.* When do I ever not think about the team or going pro?

No. All I'm consumed with as I trudge home from my ruined night is how much I want Gabe to be okay and how I need to be the one to make it okay.

———

By morning, I've calmed down. I have a thorough shower and get dressed, rolling things over in my head. Then I text the group chat, saying that I hope Gabe is okay, I'm sorry we spooked him, and that we're here when he's ready. Then I message Marty separately.

*Meet me at Toe Beans in 20 mins*

*Why?*

*Just do it, asshole*

I add a crying with laughter face so, hopefully, he knows I'm just joshing. I might have been pissed at him last night, but with some perspective, I can see that, just like me, he didn't mean to hurt or scare Gabe at all and was equally upset after he bolted.

I shove my feet into my hiking boots and grab a backpack on my way out my door to raid the frat house fridge. Fifteen minutes later, I arrive at Paddle Creek's best coffee shop, feeling jittery before I've even had any caffeine. A really big part of me wants to go back to Gabe's dorm room and bang on his door until he lets me in. But I can't do that until I have a plan of action, and to do that, I need Marty.

It's funny. He stopped being Quinn yesterday evening. I think that's telling me something right there.

A couple of minutes later, the big guy comes strolling around the corner. He gives a small, lackluster wave and smiles when he sees me, but it doesn't reach his eyes.

Yeah. He's worried about Gabe as well. I'm glad we're on the same page.

"Hey, bro," he says with a nod. "You okay?"

I shrug. "I will be, I reckon. I was hoping you'd join me on a quick hike. I figured we should talk."

Wow. His face really lights up at that. "Yeah, man. I think that's a great idea. You wanna talk about Gabe?" I nod. "Good, yeah, good."

That's not all I want to discuss, but we should wait for the rest until we have some privacy.

"Coffee?" I say with a jerk of my thumb toward the café.

"Yeah, sure!" he cries. "But I'll get it. You got the Uber last night."

He claps my shoulder and almost sends me flying. No wonder he's our best linebacker. He really is powerful.

I try not to let my mind wander off, imagining how best he could be using that power.

I follow him inside Toe Beans and can't help but grin. This place has been up and running for a couple of years now. When a huge, scary biker dude known only as Nim took over the lease, people feared that the only decent coffee house in town would get turned into a sleazy pool bar or something.

When Nim subsequently moved in over a dozen adorable rescue kitties to create a cat café, he might as well have started printing money. You have to book for weeks in advance to get a table among the cozy armchairs, doilies, and antiques. The tea and coffee selection is second to none, Nim bakes a varying selection of pastries and cakes fresh on the premises every day, and best of all, the cats are all up for adoption. He's probably found over a hundred forever homes for these little guys over just a couple of years.

Luckily, you don't need to book to walk in for takeout,

and it's early enough that the line isn't spilling out the door yet. As we wait to order, a sweet little black-and-white kitten winds their way between our legs, meowing loudly. Marty picks them up to pet them, and he looks pretty comically humungous in relation to the tiny cat. Obviously, he doesn't care.

A young woman with pale skin and copper hair is cheerfully serving everyone without missing a beat, even when Nim stomps out and slams a fresh batch of almond croissants onto the counter. He'd probably seem quite intimidating with the scowl he's wearing, but the ginger tabby wrapped around his shoulders paints a different picture.

It took me a while to trust the food here, but Toe Beans always manages to get impeccable health and safety ratings, so I gave up trying to resist the lure. There might be cats everywhere, but whatever Nim does back in the kitchen, the food remains unsullied.

When it's our turn, I get a cappuccino, Marty gets a mocha, and we both grab a bear claw each. It takes a minute to pry the black-and-white kitty away from Marty, but eventually, we end up back outside, and I'm leading him off the main street, down several side streets, then finally onto a woodland path I discovered sometime my sophomore year.

We don't talk as we move. We just sip our drinks and finish off the pastries. I've walked this path more times than I could possibly count, so my feet know the way. It's strange, though, having someone else by my side.

As we emerge out into the secluded bank by the creek this town is named after, Marty gasps. I have to admit I had the same reaction when I first discovered this little alcove. The small pebble shore reaches back under a rocky outcrop that provides both shade and shelter. The shallow river happily rushes past us, misty droplets creating rainbows as it sprays over medium-sized boulders. Birds sing their songs in the many trees around us that rustle in the gentle breeze, and the early autumn sunshine beats happily down overhead.

I turn and arch an eyebrow at Marty.

"If you tell anyone on the team about this, I *will* kill you, and they'll *never* find the body."

He drops his head back and laughs. His Adam's apple bobs in his throat, and something stirs within me. God, I could almost lick that stretch of skin.

I shake myself. "I mean it," I grumble. "This is my spot." I throw my backpack off and pull out the properly lined picnic blanket that also no one else knows about. Trust me, after sitting on these pebbles for a couple of hours, I appreciate the thick waterproof underlining, and I don't care how fussy it might seem.

"You bring hook-ups here?" Marty teases, grinning from ear to ear as he drops down onto the blanket.

I shrug and start pulling out the snacks I packed as well as the beer cans. "I've never brought anyone here before."

I try not to look up too obviously at his reaction, but he's so large I can't help but notice him freeze for a second. Yeah, big man. This is special. Don't make a huge fucking deal out of it, though.

It's stupid, but something in me warms when he points to my stash and laughs. "Day drinking. I like this coping mecha-nism." I like that he was able to follow my lead intuitively.

"Good," I say as I throw my ass down onto the blanket. "Because we have a lot of shit to sort out, and this is where I come to sort the shit out." I pass him a beer and tap my can to it. "We don't leave until things are fixed."

Marty nods, taps back, then cracks it open. The cans obviously got a little jostled on the walk up because it foams all over his hand. Something else entirely fizzes through me as I watch him grin and lick his fingers clean.

Yeah. We got a fuckton of shit to discuss.

First, though, I check my phone. Gabe's responded finally, but he's just sent a simple heart emoji, which doesn't tell me all that much. At least he isn't ignoring us or—worse—left the group chat entirely.

"Yeah," says Marty with a sigh, presumably already having seen it. "We really spooked him last night."

I chew my lower lip before taking a sip of beer. "I really like him, Marty."

I can tell he notices I didn't call him 'Quinn,' but he just raises his eyebrows for a second then takes a mouthful from his own can. "I know. But you know I like him as well, right?"

"I figured," I say with a shrug. "If we're being honest, I think we've both liked him from the beginning." He hums. I take that as a yes, even though I pretty much already knew the answer with or without his confirmation. "Okay, then... what are we going to do about it?"

Marty picks up a pebble and throws it into the creek. The sunshine sparkles in the ripples it leaves in its wake. "Nothing if Gabe doesn't want to." I study him for a moment until he looks back at me. "What?"

I shake my head. "No. It's just...I expected you to fight me for him or crack a joke. I like that your only concern is for him first and foremost."

He frowns and plays with the tab on his can. "You don't think much of me, do you?"

"I used to think you were an idiot who never took anything seriously," I tell him candidly. "But that's not who you are at all." Fuck it. If we're having a heart-to-heart, I want to keep digging and understand him better. "Why do you do that?"

"What?"

"Act the fool? Because it pisses me the hell off, and I kind of hate it even more now, knowing it was all an act."

I figure he'll tell me to fuck off or laugh, but he sits there thinking for a while. "I'm not like you, Seth," he says eventually. "You seem to have it all together. To know everything."

Before I can tell him just how wrong that is, he closes his eyes and looks pained, so I shut my mouth and continue listening. He exhales and stares over the water as he keeps talking.

"My family is amazing. Just the best. I'm in the middle of a whole herd of kids and our momma and pops raised us right. Grammy and Gramps live with us on the farm as well, and I didn't have no hesitation coming out to any of them." He throws another pebble, this one with a lot more force. "I come from a small town in Texas. Folks were okay, but they expect the gay kids to be in the theater, you know? To stay in their lane. If I wanted to keep playing football, I had to find a way to do it and not break their brains." He shakes his head and chugs down some more beer. "So class clown it was. If I was making people laugh, then they felt safe. It was like everyone knew I was gay, but if they didn't have to see it, that was allowed. I didn't even go to my prom. Not that I'd have had a date anyway. I faked a knee injury. My family threw me a party instead, but...yeah. I missed out."

Damn, that's so sad. I get it. I do. But something's bothering me. "You kept up the tomfoolery when you came here," I clarify. "Why?"

He puffs his cheeks out and shrugs. "I didn't want to, but I was nervous. I didn't know anyone, and making the guys laugh was the quickest way to make friends. Then suddenly, that's who I was, the years passed, and...well, here we are."

I hum, taking a moment to drink and reflect. "I like this Marty much better, just so you know."

The big lug gives me an adorable grin. "Really? That, um, means a lot to me, bro. I hated that I got under your skin so much." He rolls his eyes. "Naturally, that just made me prank *harder* because brains aren't my strong suit."

He laughs, and I join in. "Dumbass," I mutter, but it doesn't have any heat to it, and he hears that. But he is dumb. If I'd known him for who he is three years ago, we could have been buddies.

Maybe more.

"Come here," I say. I get to my feet and brush off my jeans.

He frowns up at me. "Where?"

I laugh and shake my head. "Here! Stand up before I change my mind."

He's still frowning, but he looks amused as he gets off the blanket and comes over to where I've moved to the middle of the shore between the alcove and the water. I get out my phone and quickly search for a playlist to stream. I'm not usually one to set the scene—I'm typically more about fucking than loving—but this is different.

I find a song by one of those cute British guys with a guitar, and hit play. It's not loud as I slip it back into my pocket, but it's enough that we can hear it in the peace and quiet of the woods. He's looking at me warily, so I sigh and beckon to him.

"You said you didn't get a prom, and that made me sad and shit, so I'm going to dance with you now, all right?"

His eyes go wide, and for a second, I wonder if I've totally missed the mark. But no. My big linebacker is a romantic at heart, I could tell. He bites his lip and steps closer to me, lifting his own arms and slotting against me. He's taller than me, but he lets me lead, and I think that's the way we both like it.

"I like you, Seth Eisen," he says softly.

I swallow as we gently rock back and forth, slowly turning to the music. "I think I might like you as well, Marty Quinn. But I also like our little Gabe. A *lot.*"

"Me, too," he agrees.

"So where does that leave us?"

He licks his lips and tilts his head as he considers me. "Why don't we ask the little dude if he likes us both as well. If so…maybe we could make it work?"

I feel my eyebrows rise. It's not an entirely foreign concept. And there was a part of me that had to be considering it. Otherwise, I would have been trying to decide between Marty and Gabe rather than bringing Marty to my special, secret spot to talk it through.

"Three of us?" I clarify.

"If you like," he says with a blush, and glances away. "If that's what he wants. It…it's what I want. At least to try. Last night…I felt it."

I squeeze his hand, and he looks back at me. I hold his gaze for a second, then allow myself to relax and smile. "I felt it, too. It was amazing."

His face lights up. "Right?" he says eagerly. However, then he looks crestfallen. "But we scared Gabe off."

"Hey." I take my hand off his hip and cup his face. "You said it last night. We'll make it right. This afternoon. We'll leave here and go get him, okay? He deserves to be looked after by us after we fucked up."

He nods, but then something devilish flashes across his features. "Ohh, he said he was a virgin, right? Maybe *we* could tutor *him* for once."

The way he waggles his eyebrows makes me burst out laughing. "Sex lessons?" I ask dubiously.

"Yep," he replies, sounding very pleased with himself. "I've had a lot of practice. I'm really good at it. I know you've had a lot of ass as well, so I assume you know what you're doing."

"Oh," I scoff. "I'm fucking amazing in bed, mister. If anything, I'm going to be teaching you *both* more than a few things."

"Yeah?" he asks, his tone challenging. "How do I know you're not just full of it? You could be all talk."

If there's one thing I love, it's a challenge.

"Enough talking," I say with a grin as I lean up and press his mouth to mine.

65

# CHAPTER 9

## Marty

It takes a second for my brain to catch up with my mouth…literally.

Seth Eisen is kissing me. He's actually *kissing me.* When the news flash finally hits me, I surge forward and bash our chests together. He's got his hands on either side of my jaw. I grab his back and get a fistful of light brown hair as my tongue clashes with his. He's a fierce kisser. I'm not exactly surprised. I've seen the way he throws his heart and soul into every game. I figured sex would be the same. But there's guessing something, and then there's experiencing it firsthand.

I'm very much enjoying my lesson so far.

"Maybe not shit?" I tease him as I break away and gasp for air.

He growls and pushes me back toward the little cave where we were chilling out. I could stop him if I wanted to. Hell, I could pick him up pretty easily. But I get a real kick out of him bodily making me back up where he wants me. I like him calling the shots. It's making me pretty fucking hard already.

He shoves me down onto the blanket. I knock my beer can over but don't care as it drains into the pebbles. I'm far more interested as Seth drops on top of me and straddles my lap, claiming my mouth again for a brutal kiss.

I can feel he's hard through his jeans, especially when he grinds down on top of me. "What are we learning today?" I ask as he bumps our noses together and then nips at my lower lip.

"How to shut up and come," he says as he pulls at my T-shirt.

I laugh and help him yank it off. We've seen each other naked a thousand times, but there's something very different in the air right now between us.

"I like this study plan," I say, unable to stop messing around.

I can't help it. I'm just so happy. And I know I just explained to him why I goof off, but it's not all entirely an act. I do like having fun and making people smile. So a thrill rushes through my body as he smirks in spite of himself.

"You're a dick."

I take his hand and shove it against my crotch. "Nah. That's my dick, darlin'."

His grin is savage. "Monster cock," he rasps, and he kisses me again and gropes me through my denim. He's not wrong. I've got a big one, and I know how to use it. I feel myself flush with pride and excitement, wondering what he wants to do with it. He's radiating top energy, but he might like to top from the bottom.

We haven't got any lube or condoms, though, unless he's hidden some away in his bag. But I get the feeling he wasn't exactly expecting to bring me up here to fuck.

There are still plenty of other ways we can get off. At least, I really hope so.

He breaks apart to shuck his flannel off. As he does, I grab his T-shirt and shove it upward. In a few seconds, we're both naked from the waist up, and his skin feels deliciously hot against mine as he pins me to the ground to kiss me some more.

He's fucking ripped. Don't get me wrong. I love how I look. I know I'm fit, but my job is to be big and get in the way of the opposing team. So my chest is kind of soft and hairy. His abs are so hard, though, and I moan as I run my hands over the smooth bumps and dips. He has some hair trailing between his pecs and below his belly button, but that's it. I like that we're different.

In turn, he grabs at my chest and pinches my nipples, making me shiver and gasp between messy, hungry kisses. It's clear we're both desperate for more, desperate for release, and it's not long before he's pawing at the zipper on my jeans.

"Get it out," he commands against my lips. "Free the beast."

I chuckle. "You want me to unleash the kraken?"

"Just do it," he says, working on his own jeans.

Yeah, I had a feeling I'd enjoy being bossed around by Seth Eisen, and I was right. My blood is pumping fast, and my skin feels like it's on fire as I hasten to do what he says and shove my pants and underwear down to my thighs. He does the same before dropping back down on me, grinding our hard, leaking cocks together.

"Fuck, yeah," he pants into my mouth. "Gonna make you come."

He forces his hand between us to wrap it around both our lengths. It's messy and kind of uncoordinated, but it's getting me off regardless. I thrust into his grip, loving how his not-unimpressive cock slides against mine. I slap my hands on his ass cheeks and squeeze hard, encouraging him to rut on top of me like an animal.

"You like that?" he practically snarls as his hand flies over our dicks. There's precum dripping onto my belly, and, yeah, I have to say I love it.

"Fuck, yeah," I gasp before dragging his lower lip between my teeth. Then I kiss up his throat and bite his earlobe. "Make us come."

He props himself up with his free hand then gets serious about jerking us off as he stares into my eyes. My breath hitches, and I find I can't look away. He's so intense. It's like I'm under a microscope, but I kind of like it.

I've been craving his attention for over three years. Now that I have it, I need every last second of it. I have no idea what's going to happen between us moving forward, but I know that I'm going to remember this breakthrough between us for years to come.

I dig my fingers into his ass cheeks and bite my lip as my orgasm begins to peak. He's grunting and dripping sweat onto me. Our musk fills the little alcove, and I love that we're practically out in the open. I know it's a secluded spot, but the fact that anyone could catch us sends a surge of lust through me.

Seth Eisen is having sex with me, mother fuckers. That's right. Drink it in.

"Fuck, Marty. *Fuck.*"

He's never called me Marty before today. It's always been Quinn. That moves something in me, and I jolt up, grabbing the back of his neck to crash his mouth onto mine. I kiss the shit out of him as I whine, my climax rushing toward me.

He lets go of his own cock and just focuses on mine, pulling back to watch me again. "Come for me, Marty," he says. I loved the fierceness from before where he was being kind of mean. But the tenderness in his voice now and the fact that he's taking care of just me are what tip me over the edge. I roar as I start spurting all over his hand and my chest, screwing up my eyes and gasping for breath.

It feels like it lasts forever, but I guess it's less than a minute until he's milking the last drops from me and I'm floating back down to earth from the heaven I just experienced. He captures my mouth for a more sensual kiss as he releases my softening cock and takes himself back in hand. It doesn't take long before he's gushing over me as well, and the mess is glorious.

I watch him as he pants for air, coming down from his high. I can't lie. I'm a little anxious how things are going to be between us now the heat of the moment has cooled off. But then he slips his hand around the back of my neck and kisses me firmly.

"*Yes,*" he hisses into my mouth.

I swallow and look into his eyes. "We okay?"

He grins and looks a bit giddy. "I think that's been building for weeks. I'm good, big man."

"Weeks," I scoff. "Try years."

He bites his lip and rakes his gaze over me. I literally just came, but that one look makes my blood hot again.

"You been jerking off over me?"

I scoff. "Come on," I protest. "You know you're hot."

He surprises me again by cupping the side of my face and caressing his thumb over my cheekbone. "I'm sorry I never gave you a fair chance before."

I mimic his gesture, feeling his stubble against my palm. "It wasn't the right time. We needed our little angel to bring us together."

Seth nods and brushes his nose against mine. "Well, now that we know we're compatible, shall we go see what he thinks about this development?"

I look between us and laugh. It's loud in the quiet of the wilderness but oddly freeing.

"I think we might need to clean up first. Otherwise, we'll scare him again."

"Oh, no," Seth deadpans as he rolls his eyes. "If only we had something to wash ourselves with."

I laugh again and shove him off, immediately sliding my jeans and briefs down my legs as I kick off my sneakers. "Last one in the creek is a rotten egg!"

Seth barks out a laugh. "That the best you can do? Last one in the creek does *shots,* I think you'll find."

We both scramble out of our clothes and across the pebbled shore. He's the fucking star quarterback, so of course he beats me, but it doesn't feel like I've lost.

In fact, as we frolic around naked in the cold water, laughing our asses off and splashing each other, I feel like I've won the jackpot.

The only thing that could possibly make this better is if our adorable little dude wants to join in on this crazy plot twist.

God, I hope so.

Or should I say *gods,* I hope so?

# CHAPTER 10

## Gabe

Welp, that's it. My life as I know it is over. I should just crawl into a hole until I graduate. Or better yet, go home with my tail between my legs.

I keep replaying that moment over and over again in my head as I lie on my bed and try and block out my awful roommate's terrible music. The panic I felt at the time was so unbelievably strong. I was genuinely terrified.

But now, I'm not sure what of.

Before my stupid brain messed everything up, I was floating in a state of bliss. No boy—no *man*—has ever touched me like that in my life. It was electrifying.

But then it was like I couldn't breathe. In a flash, it's like I saw a montage in my mind of all the ways getting close like that could go terribly wrong. I've been so incredibly grateful and awestruck to have Seth and Marty in my life. I know I was tutoring them, but it felt like we were sort of becoming friends as well.

Now I've ruined everything.

I was thankful they left me alone last night. I couldn't bear to see them or even talk to them via text. But my heart exploded in my chest when I saw Seth's message to the group this morning, and my emotions scattered all over the place. I wanted to say I was sorry and beg them both to forgive me. I wanted to pretend like it never happened and carry on like nothing had changed.

I wanted to see if they'd consider dancing with me like that again.

Instead, I just sent a heart emoji, then hid under my duvet until my roommate finally left. Then I watched stupid TikToks of kittens until I drifted back off to sleep.

I'm woken by my message alert noise. I made sure to text Mama this morning so she wouldn't worry, but I always try and keep it on noisy these days unless I'm in the library or in class, so I don't miss her calls again. It helps if I let her know when I'm going into a lecture so she'll know she can't reach me for the next hour or whatever.

I told a bit of a lie this morning and said I wasn't feeling well, so was going to probably sleep most of the day. I just wasn't sure how I'd be able to talk to her without giving away that something was up. But I resign myself that she's probably asking me to call her when I reach over and pick up my phone.

It's not my mom.

My heart leaps into my throat when I see it's another message from Seth.

*Hey, little cutie,* it reads. *Marty and I have talked, and we're really worried about you. We know we upset you last night, and we hate that. We're so sorry. Do you think you could come over to my place, where we can all talk? We'd love to apologize in person and make this right. Let me know what you think.*

The message ends with a heart emoji just like the one I sent earlier. I reread the text over and over again, not quite believing what I'm seeing. *They're* apologizing to *me?* How's that right? I'm the one who acted like a freak when they were just having fun.

Because I've thought about this. A lot. Obviously, they weren't flirting. That would be ridiculous. No. They were just messing around and blowing off steam. Then *I* was the one who read it all wrong, physically pushed them away, then blurted out that I was a frigging virgin.

How. Mortifying.

I nibble my lip and reread the message a couple more times. Maybe he's trying to help me save face and pretend like it never happened or rewrite what really did happen. A sudden thrill of hope jolts through me. If things could go back to the way they were…

*You don't have to apologize,* I say sincerely with a timid smiley face. *But I'd love to talk through everything. When should I come over? What's your address?*

The second I press send the little notification appears to let me know that Seth is typing. Then his address pops up.

*As soon as you can, bubbelah.*

I swallow and look down at myself. I'm still in the clothes I wore to Creams, having slept in them. That won't do.

I work on autopilot to shower and get dressed into something new. If I focus on brushing my teeth and picking out socks, I don't have to think too hard about the fact that Seth has invited me over to the *frat house* he lives in with a bunch of other guys on the football team.

The only thing that stops me from bailing entirely is knowing that Marty is going to be there as well. I realize in that moment that Seth called him Marty instead of Quinn in the messages just now. Also, he said 'we' about pretty much everything. Like they're a team.

That's all I've wanted since the beginning of this arrangement. If nothing else, if Seth and Marty have healed their grievances and made friends, I'll call that mission accomplished.

And if they graduate. Can't forget that part.

I'm a bundle of nerves as I make the journey over campus to where the frat houses are clustered. I'd love to belong to one of them someday, but they're mostly sports related. I just love the idea of having a family of brothers like that.

As I walk, I relisten to one of my favorite podcasts about everyday life in ancient Greece. This one's about agriculture and farming techniques, but my favorite part is about Demeter, the goddess of earth and grains, and how her daughter, Persephone, was stolen by Hades, the god of the underworld.

I know I probably shouldn't find kidnapping sexy, and there's probably something really wrong with me, but I like how these days people online generally seem to agree that Hades was absolutely whipped by Persephone. *That's* what's sexy to me. She wasn't helpless at all. In fact, she had all the power, and he was completely devoted to her.

I wish I felt even just a tiny bit powerful as I approach the frat house. I raise my eyes to the sky as I stop the podcast and put my earbuds away. "I wish I could be like you, Persephone," I whisper. "If you've got even a scrap of bravery lying around, I wouldn't mind a little of it."

I imagine her looking down on me and taking pity on the mere mortal, but it's only enough to keep my feet moving. By the time I reach the front door of Seth's house—Alpha Zeta Kappa—I'm shaking so badly I can't muster up the strength to press the doorbell.

So I'm standing on the dilapidated porch that still has a couple of tattered Fourth of July decorations lingering on it. I start thinking about how with a sand-down and a fresh coat of paint it actually wouldn't look so bad. Maybe they could add a couple of potted plants.

Then I remember this is the Paddle Creek Panthers I'm

thinking about, not a grannies gardening club. I huff and hug myself, trying to stop myself from trembling. But to my absolute horror, the door suddenly opens.

It's Duke West—Dukey—the Panthers' center. He's stunningly gorgeous. Tall, dark skin, chiseled jaw, very lickable abs that he currently has hidden under a T-shirt. Oh, gods. Is this house going to be full of people whose Instagrams I follow?

My jaw drops as he raises his eyebrows. "Hey, man," he says in a friendly enough tone. But I also get the impression that they probably get weirdos stalking around here from time to time. "Can I help you?"

I make a croaking noise before shaking my head and taking a deep breath. "M-my name is Gabriel Visoth. I'm here to see Seth Eisen, and I think Marty Quinn."

Dukey's whole expression changes. "Oh! *Gabe.* Yeah, Seth said you'd be swinging by. Come on in. His room is on the top floor. Do you need me to show you the way?"

I'm so stunned that I'm speechless for a second. Seth told people I was coming over? "No," I say, then catch myself. "No, *thank you.* I'm sure I can find my own way. Am I all right to head in?"

Dukey smiles and holds the door open for me as he steps out onto the porch. "Sure thing, man. Maybe I'll catch you later."

I step inside as he jogs down the porch, and feel apprehensive all over again. What if I meet anyone else and they think I've broken in to snoop or something? But then I spy the rainbow flag hanging to the right of the entrance hallway, and some of my nerves melt away. There are other gay and bi guys on the team. I think there's even a trans guy. Coach Drevin is openly gay and therefore the Panthers attract queer players from all over the country. I wonder if they all live in this house. Is it a rainbow fraternity, perhaps?

Knowing that I'm once more among my people, I head up the stairs with a little more confidence. When I almost bump into another guy on the second floor, I squeak that I'm Gabe here to see Seth, and he happily points me up the next flight of stairs.

I'm worried I'll know which door is Seth's, but when I get up to the landing, I realize that there's only one to choose from. Wow. He literally has his own floor.

Taking a deep breath, I walk up to it and make myself knock before I can chicken out. As soon as I do, there are noises through the wood that sound like a baby elephant having a dance party. But then the door flies open, and Marty is there, breathless and grinning at me.

"Little dude!" he cries as he yanks me into a crushing hug. "You made it."

He rubs my back and rests his cheek against my hair. When we start rocking slightly, I hear Seth clear his throat.

"Oh, right," Marty says sheepishly as he lets me go. "Yeah, sorry, Seth."

He steps aside and closes the door. As he does, Seth moves forward and opens his arms. "Would it be okay if I hugged you?" he asks.

I can't stop my eyebrows from rising. That's awfully considerate of him. I didn't mind Marty sweeping in and enveloping me. That's just his way. But Seth asking for permission rather than simply doing what he wants makes me feel kind of strange.

Almost powerful.

"O-of course," I stammer.

Whereas Marty rushed me and almost bowled me over, Seth steps calmly up to me and slowly wraps his arms around me. I can't help but melt against him, sliding my hands up his back and resting my face against his shoulder.

He smells fresh and woodsy, with a hint of cool minty shower gel. I breathe in deeply, feeling like I've come home.

I decide that I don't want to rehash last night. I don't want things to be weird. I just want to get back to how it was. So as he releases me, I smile and try and relax my tense body. "Did you want to go over those verb tables we were working on yesterday?"

Marty's laugh is startled more than anything. Seth gives him a patient but firm look, and Marty throws his hands up as he regains his composure.

"We're not studying today," Seth tells me warmly.

I feel the panic start to rise in me. I desperately try and quash it down, but I struggle. I really just want to forget about how I told two of the coolest guys on campus that I'm a big old virgin and then ran away from them as fast as I could.

"Oh, but—" I try and protest.

"We're not studying," Seth says in a tone that makes my insides turn to liquid.

Wow. I want to do anything he says in that voice.

"We're here to talk about us. All three of us."

I frown and look between him and Marty. Right. I guess completely ignoring what happened is off the table, but I can at least try and do some damage control.

"If this is about last night, I'm so sorry. I freaked out. I never should have said that or run away. That was so rude. We can just forget about it. In fact, that would probably be best, don't you think? I—"

"Hey, hey, shhh, bubbelah," Seth interrupts.

He takes one of my hands in his, then perches on the edge of his bed. I haven't even looked at his room, but a quick glance around shows me a hell of a lot of teal-and-purple Panthers' stuff as well as other teams that I guess he played on growing up. His bed is huge, and there's a big skylight that must be amazing for stargazing at night. I guess one of the perks of being the star of the football team is that you get the best room.

He gives my hand a little tug to bring my attention back to him. As I look back into his green eyes, Marty hops over and sits beside him.

Now they're both looking at me. It doesn't matter that their expressions are warm or that Seth entwines our fingers and strokes his thumb against my palm. I'm very nervous again.

"You don't have anything to apologize for," he says. Marty nods eagerly in agreement. *"We're* sorry. We came on too strong. That wasn't fair."

Marty holds up his hand like he's swearing on a Bible. "Our bad, little dude."

"We just really like you."

I need a second to allow Seth's words to sink in. My heart is starting to race. "I like you, too," I manage to say evenly. "I'm glad we're friends. That's why I shouldn't have freaked out last night. I know you were only messing around—"

"We weren't," Seth says calmly.

I blink. Then I swallow. "You…weren't?"

They both shake their heads, and then to my complete disbelief, Marty takes my other hand and cups it between both of his own.

"We were flirting with you," he says like that isn't the craziest thing in the entire world.

I can't help it. I blurt out the first word that comes to mind.

*"Why?"*

They both laugh, but it's not unkind at all. In fact, it's warm, and they both start gently caressing my hands simultaneously.

"Because you're a cutie, cutie," Marty says with a wink.

"Because you're kind, selfless, smart, and, oh yeah, totally adorable," Seth adds with a grin.

I shake my head. I'm still not getting something. Are they expecting me to…kiss them or something? Which one?

"You like me?" I say slowly and uncertainly. Because this is the star quarterback and the best linebacker of the Paddle Creek Panthers, after all. And I'm a geeky nobody. A mere mortal in the presence of the gods.

They nod. "We do," Seth says sincerely. He then looks at Marty with an affection I've never seen before. "We like each other, too." He then interlocks their two hands that are next to each other on the bed.

I stare. They're holding hands. They almost came to blows the night we first met. Now they're holding hands. And they're still holding *my* hands.

"I don't understand," I admit. My head is swimming.

Seth looks back at me with tenderness in his eyes. "We have a proposition for you, bubbelah. If you're interested?"

I have no idea what's going on. But I *do* know that this time, I'm not running away.

"I'm listening," I tell them.

There's no going back now, I guess.

# CHAPTER 11

## Gabe

"WHY DON'T YOU COME SIT DOWN?" SETH ASKS. HE LETS Marty's hand go and shifts a little over on the mattress. Then he taps the bed.

He wants me to sandwich between them again.

My pulse quickens, and my mouth goes dry. It didn't end well the last time I was their filling. But this isn't sexy dancing. It's just sitting. So I swallow and nod. They let go of my hands so I can turn and sit myself down.

But Marty immediately takes my hand again, and Seth slips his arm around my lower back, holding on to my hip.

I freeze.

"Is this okay?" Seth asks, obviously noticing right away.

My mouth moves, but nothing comes out at first. "I still don't understand," I manage to whisper.

"It's all right, darlin'," Marty says, gently rubbing the back of my hand. "We just want to take care of you, that's all."

"We both really like you," Seth says, his voice a low rumble.

It's not that authoritative tone that made my knees go weak, but there's still an element of no-nonsense about it.

Like I can't question what he means by that like I really want to, because clearly that's insane.

"We're attracted to you," he explains further when I can't make my throat cooperate to respond. "And we know what you said last night. It's okay. We don't mind if you don't have any experience. In fact, that's kind of cool."

That jerks me out of my trance. I snap my head up and frown at him. "It is?"

He grins, and my insides turn to liquid as his eyes flick up and down me. "Yeah, baby. Knowing that no one else has touched you."

"I've never even kissed a guy before," I manage to utter. Marty groans beside me like that's super sexy. I don't understand. That's embarrassing, isn't it?

"Do you want to kiss me?" Seth asks, his gaze on my mouth. "Or Marty?"

I swallow. "I have to choose?"

He shakes his head. "You don't have to kiss either of us. But if you could, would you want to? We're both here for you."

For a moment, we lock eyes. His breath is ghosting over my lips. He and Marty are radiating heat. They smell so ridiculously good. "I-I like you both," I finally stammer. "I don't want to choose."

Rather than be upset, Seth grins in relief, and Marty nuzzles his nose against the back of my neck with a hum.

"That's what we were hoping you'd say," Marty tells me.

"You don't have to choose, angel," Seth says. "We want to take care of you together. Like we already said, we like each other, too."

To my surprise, he leans forward in front of me. Marty copies him, and…

Oh my gods. *They kiss.*

It's one of the hottest things I've ever seen, and it's

happening inches away from my face. I know my jaw is hanging open, but there's nothing I can do about that.

However, as they break apart, there's still that horrible, persistent voice in the back of my mind that won't relent.

"You're two of the hottest guys on campus," I protest weakly. "What on earth do you see in me?"

"We already told you," Seth says in that sexy voice. "But if we need to give a little demonstration to convince you, then we're okay with that."

"You don't have to do anything," I squeak.

"No, we don't," Seth agrees. "We *want* to, though. We *want* you. If you want us. Just say the word, and we can tutor you for a change."

"But I'm not…"

"Nuh-uh, little dude," Marty says, squeezing my hand to make me look at him. "You're gorgeous. That's not the issue here. Seth asked what you wanted, and you need to answer him honestly. Listen to Daddy."

My eyes go wide, and I feel Seth stiffen beside me. "Daddy?" I whisper.

Wow, that's…wow. Why is that so hot?

Marty looks like he's just shocked himself with the word as well. But then he grins and shrugs. "Yeah. Daddy. Why not? He's the one in charge, and he's really good at it." He waggles his eyebrows at me. "Unless…"

"No, I like Daddy," says Seth with a peculiar tone to his voice. He touches my chin and encourages me to look at him. "Do you want to be a good boy for your Daddy and Papa?"

I'm trembling, and my *you-know-what* feels like it could explode in my jeans. I feel like I've fallen into a porn movie, except this is about a hundred times hotter. "Yes, Daddy," I say in a very small voice, trying it out. I love the feeling that Seth is in charge and wants to take care of me.

Oh, gods. They both really want to kiss me, don't they? Does that mean they want to do other stuff as well?

"What do you say to Marty?" Seth practically growls.

Oh, yeah. They asked if I was interested in them both.

I turn, feeling lightheaded. "Yes, Papa," I say to him.

He's practically bouncing with excitement. "Hell, yeah, little dude. You want us to take care of you now? We've got so many things we can teach you."

Seth laughs gently and rubs my thigh. "Don't scare him," he says warmly to Marty, but he's also being serious. I look back at him, and his expression is filled with such tenderness. "How about that kiss, bubbelah? You ready for your first one?"

With him? How is that even a question? My only hesitation is that I don't want Marty to be left out. But he squeezes my hand, and I realize that he's right there with me.

"Yes, Daddy," I rasp.

"Good boy," he says as he leans in.

Those words turn me to butter before his mouth even reaches mine. I had a vague awareness of Daddy kink from the internet, but I didn't think it was something I'd be interested in. Having a boyfriend seemed so impossible. The idea of having a Daddy never even crossed my mind.

Now it seems like I've got two.

My train of thought gets derailed the second Seth's lips touch mine. I've spent hours thinking about kissing. I've even practiced on the back of my hand.

But nothing could prepare me for the way Seth takes control. He molds my lips and plays with my tongue like it's a musical instrument. He knows just how much pressure to apply without overpowering me, although I'm quickly warming to the idea of him taking charge of me in many different ways.

My whole body is electrified, and my insides feel like

they're filled with butterflies. I whimper as I greedily try and take more from him, but he chuckles and pulls back with a parting peck at the corner of my mouth.

"I think your Papa needs some attention, too," he says with warm amusement. "Can he be your second kiss?"

"Yes, yes," I say eagerly as I turn to Marty. He slips his other arm around me like Seth has, hugging me to him so I'm practically straddling his lap.

"Gods, you really are an angel," Marty says reverently. I giggle, delighted how much I've already rubbed off on them with my obsession with ancient Greece and its mythology.

But my giggling fades as he captures my mouth for my second-ever kiss. Wow. It's different from Seth's technique, but still very good. Amazing, actually. He's more frantic, more excited, but that just makes me feel even more treasured.

Both these god-like men want me. And they're going to take me.

So, *so* willingly.

I thought my life was over this morning. How was I to know that actually, it was just beginning?

"Come here," Seth murmurs against my neck.

We shift up the bed. Mine back in my dorm hardly fits me, but Seth's allows us to all lie down, side by side. My heart is hammering and I'm trembling from head-to-toe. I'm trying not to be nervous, but I've got no idea what to expect right now.

Seth leans in for another kiss while Marty kisses and sucks on my neck. Their hands are traveling over my clothes, running along my sides, thighs, and over my tummy. I'm not sure where to put my own hands. Eventually, I settle on lightly gripping both their T-shirts as if that might keep me anchored.

Really, though, nothing is going to stop me from floating

away. Because this is either a dream or I think I might actually have died and gone to heaven.

Whenever Seth releases me, Marty is there waiting to take his turn to kiss me. They continue swapping until my jaw is aching and my lips are going numb. Just when I feel like I can't last any longer, they give me a break by kissing each other again, grinning the whole time.

"When did that change?" I ask, my voice unusually hoarse.

Seth laughs and runs his hand *inside* my thigh and gives it a playful squeeze. "This morning. We met up to talk about our feelings for you, then quickly realized we had some feelings for each other."

"So we did the responsible thing and had sex," Marty says with a straight face. He manages to look serious for about three seconds before he drops his head back and laughs. "I told you. Daddy Seth is good at taking charge. He swept me right off my feet."

*"He* picked *you* up?" I ask incredulously.

Marty winks. "I mean...I *let* him push me around. It was fun."

"I'll let you both do anything," I say, then blush furiously and screw my eyes shut in embarrassment. That was *needy* and *scandalous* and...and... I can't even think the word, but it starts with an 's' and ends with a 'lutty.' "I'm sorry," I whisper.

"Baby boy," Seth says firmly. He takes hold of my jaw firmly enough that it prompts me to open my eyes and look at him. "Don't ever apologize for giving consent if that's what you really want and mean. Your Daddies are here to *worship* you. We've wanted you since the moment we laid eyes on you. *We're* your Gods now."

"And you're our cherub," Marty joins in enthusiastically. He runs his fingers through my hair, then brushes his thumb over my swollen lower lip. "Sent from heaven to save us."

"Oh," I say weakly. That's like something out of a romance

novel. It's tempting to keep asking myself how this could possibly be happening, but it is, and I don't want to delay another second of it.

I came to college to further my education, yes. But I also came to finally discover who I really am and—if I was really lucky—to explore some new experiences.

I never could have imagined this scenario even in my wildest fantasies. It's time to stop second-guessing and just go with the flow. I might not have known Seth and Marty for that long, but I trust them to look after me.

"Um, okay," I say with a nervous giggle. Seth's hand is still resting on my inner thigh, so tantalizingly close to my you-know-what. "What do you want to, um, do? Daddy," I tag on at the end, just to see his reaction.

Seth's smile is positively scorching. Yeah, I think this little role play is working for all of us.

"Oh, angel," he growls, squeezing my thigh. "There's *so* much we could do for you. I want to show you everything. But I think we should go slowly to start with."

I bite my lip and nod, hoping I don't look too disappointed. I love that he's not rushing me and is respecting my inexperience. But at the same time, I've jumped into this now with both feet. I don't want to give myself the chance to chicken out.

Seth chuckles and glances at Marty. "Oh, Papa. I think our baby boy is ready for *something* at least, judging by that pout."

"I reckon so, Daddy," Marty says with a huge grin. "Tops off?"

Seth nods. "Tops off. Let's see some of that pretty body of yours, cherub."

I gasp as they both reach for the hem of my T-shirt, but just before they pull it up, Seth pauses.

"Wait," he says with slight urgency as he looks at Marty.

"We need a safe word, right? Something baby boy can say if he really wants us to stop."

"Oh, yeah," Marty agrees. "Good thinking. Uhh…"

"Olympus," I say without hesitation. They both look down at me. "It's the mountain where the gods live," I explain with a shy smile. "Like if we need to stop and go home for a minute."

"Love it," Seth says sincerely. "And if things are good, you just say 'heavenly,' yeah?"

That should be pretty easy to remember. It's how I'm feeling right now, after all. I nod.

"Should there be a middle one as well?" Marty asks with a small frown. "Like when we ask Coach Drevin for a timeout to think for a second."

"'Timeout' is fine," I say. "It'll make me feel like I'm one of the guys."

They both laugh at that, but it's sweet. Like they're indulging me for being silly and pretending I'm on the team.

"So how does this make you feel?" Seth asks, a seductive rasp to his voice as he slips his hand under my shirt and skims his palm over my tummy. I shiver and close my eyes.

"Heavenly," I groan.

Then there are two pairs of hands working together to pull the shirt up my body and over my head. My eyes flutter open as I fall back down onto the mattress, feeling the cool bedding against my back. In a flash, they both also whip their tops off, and suddenly, there's a *whole* lot of skin right in front of me.

"Oh…gosh," I say, feeling my eyes go so wide I'm worried they'll fall out of my head.

Marty chuckles. "I wonder what it'll take to make you cuss, baby boy."

I blush. "A lot," I confess. That's not how I was raised.

But Seth just hums and starts kissing up my throat. "That sounds like a challenge, doesn't it, Papa?"

"It does," Marty agrees.

Then...oh...*oh.*

Seth kisses my mouth again, but Marty leans down and wraps his lips around my *nipple.* I squeak into Seth's mouth, pawing aimlessly around with my hands to try and find some purchase on something as Marty starts to suck and lick and even *nibble* my hardening bud. Seth outdoes him, though, when his hand drifts upward and gently caresses my groin through my jeans.

"Oh, gods!" I cry out.

"Is this okay, cherub?" Seth asks, giving my bulge a little squeeze.

For a second, I can't catch my breath. But then I'm nodding like crazy. "Heavenly," I assure him.

He kisses me again as he massages that whole area. I'm disgraceful as I thrust up into his palm, but he doesn't seem to mind. In fact, I'm pretty certain he likes it a lot.

"Can we make you come, beautiful boy?" he murmurs against my lips.

I blink my eyes open and stare at him for a second. Then Marty releases my abused nipple and takes my hand in his, kissing the backs of my fingers gently as he also looks into my eyes.

"Can we worship at your altar?" he asks.

My head is spinning. I'm definitely dead. There's no way this is real. But if so...*wow,* what an afterlife.

"Please," I manage to croak. "Please, Daddies. *Please.*"

Seth's smile is so full of affection. There's still fire there, but I feel warmed by the flames, not engulfed.

He glances at Marty, then slips his hand behind his neck. He draws him down as he leans toward me as well, then... Oh, gods. They're *both* kissing my mouth at the same time.

It's messy and doesn't last long, but once again it's like nothing else I've ever experienced. To feel them both claiming me—not fighting but sharing—is something I hope I'll experience a lot more of.

When they break away, Seth raises his eyebrows at Marty. "Clothes off," he commands.

Marty grins and hops off the bed without hesitation.

I watch on, speechless, as in a flash they shove down their pants and underwear, leaving them totally naked. My head swings comically back and forth as I absorb the stunning members in front of me. They're both half-hard, and much like the rest of them, Seth is big, but Marty has a *monster* between his thighs. The idea of fitting that inside me is positively terrifying. I'm not sure I could even get the top of it in my mouth.

"Hey, little cherub," Seth says kindly, crawling back onto the bed and cupping the side of my face to get me to look at him instead of Marty's length. "We're going slowly, remember? No one's riding that beast today. We're just going to have a bit of fun. How are you feeling?"

I take a couple of breaths and dial myself back down from a timeout. "Heavenly," I assure him, placing my hand over his.

"Good boy," he says, and I glow at his praise. I want to be so, *so* good for him and Marty.

For Daddy and Papa.

Seth—no. *Daddy*—pops the button on my jeans, and I try my best not to quiver as between them they divest me of the rest of my clothes.

And then we're all naked, the three of us together.

My breathing is ragged as they snuggle up on either side of me, skimming their fingers delicately over my body.

"So fucking beautiful," Papa whispers.

"A gift for the gods," Daddy agrees. "An untouched angel."

"Daddy," I murmur as he peppers kisses against my cheek.

Papa nuzzles his nose against the side of mine. Their breaths are hot against my skin, and with every swipe of their hands they get closer and closer to *down there.* I'd deflated somewhat with nerves, but blood is pumping south now in earnest.

My...my *cock* is swelling, and I want them to touch it so badly.

But first, Daddy deftly picks up Papa's hand where he was stroking my tummy. He brings it to his mouth and sucks on the middle and index fingers. Papa and I both gasp, watching intently as Daddy gets them good and wet. Then he removes them and guides Papa's hand between my legs. Between my...

*Oh!*

I'm feeling that word that rhymes with 'lutty' again as I quickly part my knees, giving them access to my hole.

"Don't go too far," Daddy tells Papa as the first slippery finger swipes over my entrance.

"Of course," Papa says reverently.

I whimper and gasp, doing my best not to close my eyes, but the sensation is so overwhelming. I've barely touched *myself* there, and now Papa's large fingers are stroking and gently probing the tight ring of muscle.

That's nothing compared to when Daddy licks his palm, then wraps his hand around my hardening cock.

"Oh!" I yell, forgetting that there's a house full of guys beyond that door. But then I remember that we're alone on the top floor and decide not to care.

Besides, it's difficult to think of anything as Daddy starts gliding his hand up and down my length. He kisses my mouth once more, and Papa latches on to my neck. I have to close my eyes as I drown in all the sensations, whimpering noises escaping my throat, even if they can't quite make it past my lips.

I wasn't even aware of where my hands were until Daddy carefully picks up the one closest to him. "Just hold on, gorgeous boy," he says moments before he places it where he wants it.

On his cock.

I'm touching another man's cock.

Oh, gods. It feels *amazing*.

Papa quickly realizes what Daddy's done and does the same. It's like I'm suddenly gripping on to the world's sexiest handlebars. Daddy said to just hold on, and that's why I try and do as they return to pleasuring me. I attempt to jerk them both off a bit, but it's a lot, and they seem better at thrusting against my palms.

So I just try and use what little I have of my brain left to stay still and let them worship me like they wanted to. We're all rock hard now and leaking precum, making the hand jobs smooth and utterly incredible. Their cocks are solid and hot in my hands, and my own length feels ready to explode in Daddy's tender grasp. The tip of Papa's middle finger is pulsing just inside my fluttering hole.

My whole body is on fire, and I could happily die in the flames.

"Come for us, angel," Daddy murmurs. "Come all over your perfect body. Show your gods who you belong to."

His words are so insanely hot that my climax rushes over me like a tidal wave, dousing the flames in one huge surge. I scream as I start spurting over Daddy's hand and up my stomach, feeling like my soul is leaving my body.

I come and come, eventually spending every last drop. I flop against the mattress, my breath and spirit coming back to me. I'm utterly exhausted and can't muster the energy to do anything but look up at my Daddies.

They don't seem to expect me to do anything more, though.

Their hands replace where mine had been holding. As they start to jerk off over me, Daddy leans over, inviting Papa to meet him in the middle for a kiss. They make out for a few seconds as they start to pick up their pace, but then they part and look down at me as they pant and tremble, clearly reaching their peaks.

I breathe heavily, watching the hottest thing I've ever seen in my life. Two gods bearing down over a mere mortal as they lose themselves and start spilling their ambrosia all over me.

Except they said I wasn't ordinary. They called me their angel, their cherub, and as I bask in their glory covered in all our seed, I feel worshipped to within an inch of my life.

# CHAPTER 12

## Seth

I COLLAPSE BY GABE'S SIDE, AS DOES MARTY. I THINK WE'RE all a bit shellshocked at the intensity of what just happened, but I can't deny that seeing our little angel covered in all of our cum is sexy as all hell.

And…I'm Daddy now.

It's not like I don't usually take charge during sex. In fact, that's what I love the most. I find eager little twinks and call them my cum sluts as they suck my dick. I fuck them hard and make them beg. But this…

This is different.

I don't kick anyone out of my bed, ever. But there's always an understanding that when we're done, we're probably going to go our separate ways and not see each other again.

With Gabe, though, I gather him up in my arms and don't care about the sticky mess as I hug him tightly to me. "Mine," I growl. It's like a promise to myself and the universe. The idea of anyone else touching him now is unfathomable.

Anyone but Marty, of course.

I reach out and grab his hand, squeezing it as I catch his

eye. "Mine," I say again, feeling like a caveman dragging his mates back to his cave.

Marty looks like he's run a hundred laps, but he still gives me a cheeky grin. "Yes, Daddy," he says.

That's right. I am Daddy. And the difference between Daddies and a bossy bitch in bed is that Daddies take care of their boys. And their Papas if necessary.

I look down at a very sleepy Gabe, my chest bursting with pride. That was literally his first orgasm given to him by someone else, and from the blissed-out expression on his face, I think we did a very good job.

"How are you feeling, bubbelah?" I check in.

He blinks sluggishly, but a small smile tweaks at the corner of his mouth. "Heavenly, Daddy," he utters. "Beautiful."

My heart swells even bigger. "You *are* beautiful," I assure him. "Always, but especially with your Daddies' cream all over you. We've claimed you now. Like animals. You've got our scent on you, so other men know to stay away."

I'm surprised at how passionate my words are, but they're true. I squeeze Marty's hand, so he knows the same goes for him. This is my pack now. Marty is going to help me look after Gabe, and I'm going to look after them both.

If I'm a great team captain, I'm going to be the best fucking boyfriend this town has ever seen.

I catch myself and lick my lips as I look between Marty and Gabe. It's probably not the right time to bring up the B-word seeing as they're both almost comatose, but if I'm laying claim to them, then we might as well label it for what it is.

Later.

For now, I slip my arm underneath our little cherub's back and encourage him to sit up. He groans in protest, making me chuckle.

"Come on, angel," I cajole him. "We can't let that dry on you. It'll be horrible. Let's get into the shower."

"Here, I got him," Marty says. My big man scoops our boy up in his arms like a rag doll, standing and hugging him to his chest.

Fuck. He really does look like a gladiator like that, naked and cradling our precious boy.

I kneel on the bed and beckon him in for a kiss over Gabe's sleepy body. "Thank you, Papa," I tell him warmly.

He beams, and my heart aches.

It's quite frankly terrifying how much has changed between the three of us in under twenty-four hours. But we've been spending so much time together these past few weeks—we've gotten close fast, and I could feel *something* more than friendship was brewing.

This is another level, though.

I shake my head and leave Marty to carry Gabe into the en suite. I head in first to get the hot water going. It's going to be a bit of a squeeze in the tub under the shower, but we'll manage. Gabe's the one who really needs a rinse, but I want both me and Marty to do that for him together.

He's fucking adorable as Marty puts him back on his feet. He sways and blinks sleepily as I wait for the hot water to kick in. "You did so good for your Daddies, baby boy," I murmur against his cheek before I kiss his mouth gently. Marty hugs him from behind and kisses the top of his head. I catch his eye. "And you were fucking gorgeous, big man."

He bites his lip as he grins. I never thought I'd see the day he got bashful on me, but here we are.

"So were you," he says, and I hear that awe in his voice again.

I can't believe how wrong I've been about him all this time. I'm so glad he's dropped the bullshit and has let his real, authentic self start to shine through.

Between us, we get Gabe under the water and quickly wash off all our mess. I'm kind of sad to see it trickle down the drain, but then I remind myself that this was just the first time.

Who knows how many other times we're going to get together like this? A *lot,* if I have anything about it.

The hot water seems to revive our little angel back to life. He stirs and blinks, taking deep breaths as he appears to become more aware of our surroundings. We're like sardines in a can. Marty's hardly under the stream at all. But he's grinning, and so am I, and Gabe giggles shyly.

"That's better," he says. "Not that I didn't love it in the moment, but it was getting cold."

"Yeah, it'll do that if you leave it," I tell him. *Gods.* I can't wait to teach him everything I know about sex. I want to make him come in a hundred different ways. And with Marty in the mix as well, it's so exciting. I hope the big guy will let me fuck him.

I wonder if I'd want him to fuck *me* with that giant cock. There's something tantalizing about that idea. I'd still be the top, of course. But I can do that with him inside me, I'm sure.

I'm getting ahead of myself. Yes, there are so many ways in which we can all fit together. But right now, we're not thinking about fucking. This is what being a Daddy is about, I'm sure. It's about tenderness.

I turn off the water and reach for my towel. Unfortunately, I've only got the one, but I can fix that easily enough with a quick trip to the department store. For now, we dry Gabe first, then I give it to Marty before taking my turn last.

We'd planned that there might be some snuggling, so Marty brought sweatpants with him. I'm glad, as I'd have nothing that would fit him. I pull on a pair myself, but I give Gabe my favorite ones. They're my old high school pair, and they're soft with age and wear. I pull the drawstring extra tight so they won't fall down, then I drag both my guys down onto the bed again in a puppy pile with Gabe in the middle. Luckily, we got most of the mess on our boy, so we cuddle together on top of the duvet. With three of us on the bed, we're radiating heat so catching a chill isn't a worry.

"How are you feeling, baby boy?" I ask. I appreciate that between post-orgasm zombie, showering, and now, he could have three completely different responses, so I don't worry about asking again.

Besides, I'm Daddy. I do what I want.

But he turns to me and looks content. That fretful anxiety from before seems to have melted away. At least for now.

"I feel like the luckiest boy in the world," he says softly.

Marty is already hugging him, but he squeezes tighter. "I hear you, darlin'," he says. His Texas accent comes out more when he's tired, but I like it. Again, it's more of his authentic side coming through. I want him to stop hiding. He doesn't need to anymore.

Not when he's got me.

Us.

Gabe smiles up at him and laughs. "I'm sorry, but it's still crazy that you think you're lucky to have *me*. You're...like... celebrities. This whole town loves you both. You must have guys banging down your doors. Trust me, *no one* is banging on my door."

I touch my thumb and finger to his chin to make him look at me. I get a real thrill every time when he goes compliant.

"That's only because we got in there first before anyone else realized how incredible you are," I say calmly, like this is very obvious. It is to me. "Sucks to be those losers. But *that's* why we're lucky. We found you first, and now we're keeping you."

"We're your Daddies," Marty says happily.

"We're your Gods," I add, something feral uncoiling in my belly. The captain in me who's used to being responsible for the wellbeing of others knows we can't have sex again so soon. We need time to process this all.

But the man in me wants to fuck all day and night and never stop.

"Daddy Zeus," Marty quips.

I jerk my head to blink at him. "I actually like that. He *was* the father of all the Greek gods, wasn't he, cherub?"

Gabe beams at me. "I'm so proud that you remembered that," he says.

"Daddy Zeus," I say again.

"Daddy Z," Marty suggests.

"Ohh, I like *that*," Gabe says with a giggle.

I grin. "Me, too." I capture his lips for a filthy kiss. "Gonna make you scream it next time we have sex."

"Oh," he squeaks, his eyes wide. It gets my blood pumping. Yeah, there's going to be a next time.

Soon.

"A-and Marty?" he asks, deflecting the sexual tension away. I'm not surprised, but I will be training that out of him as soon as I can. He's a sexy baby, and I won't be satisfied until he knows it.

But I play along with his question for now. "Hmm," I say, thinking about what I've learned. "Ares? God of war, *grr*."

I poke Marty in the ribs, and we both laugh. I think he looks like a warrior all right. But Gabe shakes his head.

"Papa's a lover, not a fighter," he says thoughtfully. Then his expression brightens, and my heart aches with how much I love seeing him happy. "Dionysus!"

"Bless you," I say automatically.

Baby boy laughs and shakes his head. "No. Dionysus was basically the god of drinking and orgies."

Marty's jaw drops. "Fuck, *yeah!*" he cries, punching the air.

"Daddy Z," Gabe says softly, gently touching my bare chest before doing the same to Marty. "And Papa D."

I caress the side of his face. "And you're our angel, our cherub, our beautiful baby boy."

He takes a deep breath. I watch as it seems like the last trace of his resistance finally vanishes for good.

"Yes, I am," he says.

I have no idea where this is going or how long it can last if Marty and I are (supposedly) graduating next semester. I don't even know how to be a boyfriend to one guy, let alone two.

But I'm Daddy now, and I'll work it out. No matter how many bumps there are along the way.

# CHAPTER 13

## Gabe

"Okay, Mama," I say, doing my best not to sound like I'm trying to get off the phone. "I better go. I have to do some reading before class."

I'm walking through campus, feeling like everything looks particularly beautiful today. The people, the buildings, the trees. I've got a spring in my step and a grin on my face. In fact, I'm like Hermes, the messenger of the gods. I've got wings on my feet, and nothing's going to stop me from getting where I'm going.

My mother is trying her best to dampen my mood, though. "Always with your nose in a book now," she tuts. "It's not good for you. How is that going to help you run a restaurant?"

A sharp stab of fear and anxiety pierces through me, but I do my best to shake it off and force myself to smile. She can't see it, but it makes me feel better.

The idea of running that place until my parents pass away and I can sell it fills me with the kind of dread I can't adequately put into words. I have *mad* respect for them for living their dream and making such a success of it. But to me, it's going to be a prison sentence.

Hopefully, that's years away. I can't do anything about it at the moment, so I make that smile bigger and laugh. "It's *math*, Mama" I lie. I hate math, but I'm planning on taking some basic accounting and business management courses before I return home, so I'll know *something*. Not now, though.

For now, I can live in ancient Greece, at least in my mind. Especially because I have my very own Gods to worship me.

And yeah, okay. I know it's the mortals who are supposed to worship the gods, but I don't think that's going to come up in either Daddy or Papa's upcoming tests, so I'm happy to keep going with the slightly wonky metaphor.

So…*so* happy.

"Oh," Mama says, sounding mollified at my fib. "That's good, chico. You're a smart boy. I know you won't let your family down."

"Love you, Mama. Bye," I say, sidestepping her comment. There are so many ways in which I can let her down. She just doesn't know it yet.

She wishes me well and hangs up the phone. I chew my lip as I crunch over the path, my thoughts spiraling as I think about the fate that lies before me. Ever since I was a boy, my parents have pressed upon me how one day I'll inherit their beloved restaurant. I waited tables there all throughout high school, struggling to keep up with my homework but still getting my scholarship despite the odds.

It didn't occur to me until I came to Paddle Creek and got away from the daily grind if I even *wanted* to work there once I graduate, let alone if I wanted to run it. I shiver as the thought literally makes my blood run cold.

I thrive best when I'm left to my own devices. I've known such peace since leaving home. Mama means well, but I wasn't ever even allowed to close my bedroom door. She constantly interrupted me and was always getting me to help with chores and stuff, even if I was right in the middle of something. My time was never my own.

I never wanted to let her down or be selfish, of course! But sometimes, it felt like even my *thoughts* weren't mine. Which was dangerous when I had so many secrets to hide.

Here, I've been able to lose myself for hours in my beloved library. I know my roommate is annoyingly loud, but he does actually leave me alone, and when he's gone, it's bliss. I either eat in the cafeteria or outside with a book for company and go on long walks.

Sure, it was getting a bit lonely, but that was before I somehow managed to get myself *two* boyfriends. My Daddies. We're not flaunting our relationship just because it's new and a bit fragile. But Daddy hasn't been shy with the PDA in the safety of his frat house, and Papa is always picking me up and roughing up my hair. He says I have curls like an angel, and he can't seem to stop touching them.

I'm pretty sure Ms. Maude has caught on to us, but she hasn't said anything. I just noticed one day there was a collection of three crystals tucked under the table we always sit at, and the other day she mentioned something about Mercury or Venus being in retrograde or something. I'm not really sure what that meant, but she gave me a knowing nod and said that it was no wonder I was happy.

Planets or gods, I think she's right. Someone or something is shining down on me, and you better believe I'm the happiest I've probably ever been in my whole life.

Thinking of my Daddies eases my troubled mind, especially as that's where I'm headed right now, to Alpha Zeta Kappa. Telling Mama white lies has unfortunately become second nature to me, but I promise myself it's for her own good, so that makes it okay. I don't have reading to do for a class. I've just come from one. But I am going to study with my Daddies.

'Study,' ha-ha.

I am strict. We do still have to get them to graduate. So keeping our library sessions ensures we mostly behave and essays are still getting written. But we also meet up at the house a lot, and those sessions often start with good intentions, but then...

Oh, goodness. The other day they made me kneel for them while they towered over me, their big cocks pointed at my face. I'm nowhere near to deep-throating yet—although Daddy is starting to teach me—but I managed to suck the tips and jerk them off until they came all over me. They *love* doing that, and even though I know it's really dirty and naughty, I love the feeling of being covered in their seed. Daddy is right. It makes me feel claimed. Like they own me.

Another time when Daddy was training me to swallow his dick, Papa got behind me and *ate out my hole.* I'd seen rimming videos before, but I always thought it looked a bit weird. I had absolutely no idea that it could feel so amazing. I worried that it was a bit gross for him, but Papa assured me that he absolutely loves doing it. Still, I always do my best to make sure I'm as fresh as I can be for them down there before I see them. When I plucked up the courage to finally trim my hair around that area, I couldn't decide if it was debauched or hilarious.

I find myself talking more to Aphrodite than I ever have before. I even set up a little secret shrine for her among the flowers by the bench behind the library. That's where my relationship with my Daddies changed, and it seemed appropriate. Roses are her flowers, so I put a little candle under one of those bushes in the shape of a swan, as that's one of her symbols as well. I also put down some cherries the other day as an offering, but I'm basically leaving them for Clayton, the campus raccoon. Aphrodite can appreciate them until he finds them for his dinner.

I always knock to be let into the house, even though they generally leave the door open during the day. I just think it's polite. That does mean, though, that I've met most of the guys who live there now, and yes, they're all queer. I had no idea there were so many of them on the team, but it makes me really happy that there are. They've all been super nice to me, too, greeting me with a knowing grin every time.

At first, I got extremely embarrassed at the idea of them being aware of what I got up to with Daddy and Papa, but over time I've realized that's silly. Why be shy when it's one of the best things that's ever happened in my life? If anything, I now feel *proud* that even though it's all still unofficial, they know that Daddy and Papa have chosen me.

I'm theirs.

Papa's frat house is about a ten-minute drive away from here but in the opposite direction to my dorm. He's in a really wild place, but I get the feeling that now he has me and Daddy, he's suddenly over the party lifestyle.

Somehow, he's always here before I arrive and is generally the one to open Daddy's door with a big, goofy grin. Like I'm the most exciting thing he's seen all day. I keep waiting for his enthusiasm to fade, but it hasn't yet.

Not for any of us.

I know this arrangement we have can only last until graduation because after that, our lives will head in completely different directions. Heck, I'm not even sure it'll survive the Christmas break. When they come back in spring, football season will be over, and they'll have much more time to study. I don't know if they'll need me anymore.

But I do my best not to think about that and just focus on the here and now, and how incredible it is, no matter how improbable or temporary.

"Angel," Papa says as he yanks open the door, sighing like he hasn't seen me in months instead of hours. He pulls me in a hug and nuzzles his face against my hair, inhaling deeply. For someone so big and strong, he's always amazingly gentle with me.

Not like Daddy. Daddy often pushes me around and pins me down because he *owns* me, and I love it so much it hurts. But then afterward, he always holds me tight and tells me I'm perfect, and *urgh,* I don't know how I got so lucky in life.

That's what I mean. Even if this can't last, I'll still treasure it forever.

Even if it's going to hurt like hell when it all ends.

I don't think about that now, though. For today, I allow Papa to pull me into Daddy's room and lock the door behind us. From the way his hands are already all over me, I have a strong suspicion that no books are getting cracked today.

"Not studying, then?" I say, pretending to be stern, but the effect is probably ruined by my giggle.

"Oh, we're going to teach you something all right, cherub," Papa says, waggling his eyebrows as he drags me toward the foot of the bed.

Daddy was sitting at his desk, but now he's risen and come to crowd behind me, running his hands up and down my arms as he kisses the side of my neck. My heart is already racing, and I feel giddy with excitement and anticipation.

"You've been so perfect for your Daddy Gods," he mumbles against my skin, making me shiver. "You've learned so much. We think you're ready for more, and you're going to love it, little one."

"Yeah?" I manage to rasp, my mind already whirring.

More? He means *that,* doesn't he? He's got to. Oh, gods. I've been so desperate to feel them inside me, but I'm also scared. It seems like so much—especially Papa—and I'm not sure I can take it. I'd never ever want to disappoint them.

Daddy must feel me tense because he wraps his arms around me, as does Papa. They just hold me for a few moments, gently rocking from side to side. "What's your safe word, cherub?" Daddy eventually asks.

"Olympus," I say without hesitation. I haven't had to even think about using it yet, but just reminding me that I have it helps me to calm down.

He presses his lips to my fluttering pulse point. "Good boy. So good for your Daddies. Now you know Daddy and Papa went and got tested last week, yeah?"

"Yes, Daddy," I say, feeling a little calmer. They did tell me that, so this development really shouldn't be that much of a surprise to me.

"Well, the results all came back fine," he continues, "and we can't wait another minute to claim you. To have you for the first time. So how do you feel about taking your Daddies' cocks into your sweet, virgin hole, one after the other? How does the idea of getting filled to the brim with their hot, salty cum make you feel?"

I'd been on the verge of a time-out, but now I'm quivering with a frantic need. "It makes me feel like…like a naughty boy," I manage to utter.

Daddy chuckles darkly as Papa rests our temples together and moans softly, his massive hands running over my thighs and hips. I'm getting hard in my jeans, and my skin feels like it's on fire.

"Such a good little slut for your Gods," Daddy growls, nipping my earlobe. I gasp at the use of the bad word…but it doesn't feel bad when Daddy uses it like that. It actually feels really *good*. "We're going to fuck you all the way into heaven, little angel. You're going to scream our names in worship."

My breathing is ragged, and my knees are in danger of giving out. Since that first time here, I always look forward to our times at the frat house, so badly in fact it's becoming an addiction. But I'd never imagined this would be happening today on my walk over.

I'm already in heaven, but if my Daddy Gods want to give me euphoria, I'll beg for it until my voice is gone.

"Yes, Daddy," I rasp. "Please. I'll be so good for you both, I promise. I can take it."

"I know you can, cherub," Daddy says as he reaches down and squeezes my bum. "You've learned so much from your Daddies' fingers. We'll go slow. Papa is going to fuck you first, while Daddy watches, getting so hard for you. Then you're going to ride Daddy and make him come. Then your Daddies will reward you and help their sweet baby boy come all over himself. How does that make you feel?"

I'm shaking again, and my breathing is a little shallow. I want to reply 'heavenly,' but I'm stuck on one not-so-small detail.

"P-Papa's going to go first?" I whisper. I'd always assumed that when this happened, Daddy would go first to stretch me out, and *then* I'd try and take Papa. He's so huge it's making me break out into a sweat just thinking about trying to fit him inside.

Daddy turns me around and takes my chin between his thumb and finger. Papa immediately envelops me with his big, strong arms and rests his jaw on top of my head. I feel safer, but the panic is still bubbling under the surface.

"You trust Daddy, don't you, cherub?"

I nod without hesitation. "Yes, yes," I cry. "I just…I don't want to disappoint you."

"You could never," Papa says, sounding almost outraged.

Daddy chuckles fondly. "Papa D is right, angel. You could never, ever disappoint your Gods. But Daddy wants you to try and do what he asks. He wants to watch you pop your cherry, then fuck you hard and fill you with his cum. Then both your Daddies will help you tumble into the abyss of ecstasy. That's what Daddy wants. Can you give it to him?"

I breathe slowly and look into his green eyes. I trust Daddy, and I want to be so good for him and give him what he wants. He says we'll go slow.

But best of all, he wants to *watch* me. Me. Hundreds of people watch them play football almost every week. No one ever watches me.

Until now.

"I can do it, Daddy," I manage to whisper. "It sounds heavenly. I'll be your perfect angel."

He kisses me hard. I can feel his cock against my hip. "Good boy," he says, his voice heavy with lust. "Good, sweet, perfect angel."

He raises his eyes and nods at Papa. Together they make short work of undressing me.

"Lie on the bed on your back, cherub," Daddy tells me. "Rub your cock and make yourself hard and wet for your Gods."

I'm still trembling, but I'm eager to do as I'm told. As I lie back and take my already half-hard length in hand, my Daddies watch me intently as they swiftly strip themselves naked. They're definitely on their way to full hardness as well, and I do my best not to gulp as I look at the beast Papa has between his solid thighs.

I can do this, I tell myself firmly.

Daddy nods to Papa before crawling onto the bed. Papa goes and gets our bottle of lube. It occurs to me that they probably discussed this before I came over, and that soothes me further. They strategized, just like they do with football. They have a game plan, and I'm their star player.

They'd never let me down.

"Come here, baby," Daddy says as he grabs my hips. I gasp as he rolls us over so I'm now on top, on my hands and knees. "That's it. Stay just there," he tells me before he captures my lips in a burning kiss.

I moan and whimper as he strokes my cock, teasing me. The next thing I feel are Papa's hands pulling my ass cheeks apart and his hot tongue probing against my hole.

The room is filled with the wet sounds of smacking lips, groans, grunts, and my little squeaks. Daddy rubs his finger over my slit, milking precum from it and smearing it down my straining length. Papa's mouth is soon replaced by two fingers that he crooks to massage my prostate. That special, mythical spot that I'd sort of found on my own before, but there's nothing like the sensation of a red-blooded man teasing it.

Two digits become three, and Daddy bites my lip, dragging it through his teeth as he stares at me through his lashes. His breathing is heavy with lust, and I'm shaking with the effort of staying on all fours above him.

"Are you ready now, cherub? Your God, Dionysus, is going to fuck that sweet hole of yours until he comes in your ass. Daddy Zeus is going to watch you in all your glory because you're an angel slut, born to be fucked by Gods. Isn't that right?"

"Yes," I splutter, trying not to squirm in desperation. "Yes, Gods, *please.* I want to be fucked so badly. I'll be so good for you both."

Wow. Apparently, I cuss all the time now.

"Good boy," Daddy says.

He wraps his hand around the front of my neck. I can still breathe, but it reminds me that I'm *his.* I exist for his pleasure. He's going to watch me lose my virginity, and I'm so excited I could combust.

I have to be honest, though. The panic returns as soon as Papa pushes the mushroom head of his huge cock against my entrance. He's stretched me good—and has been doing so for weeks now—but I still feel impossibly full as he breaches me.

"Look at Daddy, angel," Daddy growls. I gasp and blink, but I do as he says. "You can do this. Just relax. Breathe with Daddy. That's it. Nice and deep."

Together, we inhale and exhale as Papa pushes oh-so-slowly into me. When it doesn't seem quite so impossible and I begin to relax, Daddy kisses me again and caresses my deflated cock, making me jerk and gasp into his mouth.

"Good boy," he mumbles against my lips. "You look so fucking perfect with Papa's giant God cock in you. Are you going to let him fuck you, little angel?"

"Yes, Daddy, yes," I beg.

"Of course you are," he says with a grin. "Such a beautiful slut for your Daddies. How does he feel, Papa?"

"So good, Daddy," Papa gasps. He sounds so desperate for me even though he already has me. It makes my skin tingle and my balls ache. "So tight. Such an angel."

Daddy squeezes my cock and makes me gnash my teeth. "You hear that, cherub? Already so perfect for your Daddies. I want you to fuck Papa Dionysus now. Take that enormous cock of his so deep it chokes you."

"Yes, Daddy," I hiss as Papa starts to thrust his hips. He's slow at first, but every time he slams into me, fireworks explode like the Fourth of July. This is my own private public holiday. The day I worship my Gods, and they gift me every-thing another man could possibly give me.

And I don't just mean the sex.

Although so far, that's going pretty great I have to say.

It's a strange sensation that I'm still trying to get comfort-able with, but it helps that I can cling on to Daddy as hard as I like. I'm squealing and whimpering and yelping, getting louder and louder, but my Daddies seem to love that a lot.

"Yes, baby," Daddy murmurs before sucking my earlobe.

"Scream for your Daddy Gods. Tell everyone who you're worshiping."

"Ohhh," I say, dragging out the sound as Papa pummels into me, getting faster and faster. *"Fuck,"* I eventually bellow.

Daddy grins and lets go of my dick with a final squeeze. "Do you like that?" he growls, holding tight against my neck and the side of my ribs. "Do you like Papa's big, fat cock inside you?"

"Yes, Daddy!"

"You look fucking gorgeous. Both of you. So magnificent, Papa."

"Daddy," he grunts, sounding desperate as he slams into me.

"Come, big man," Daddy says with a jut of his chin. "Come inside our sweet cherub. Fuck him so hard he cries."

I do yell out as Papa ramps it up even further, tears springing in my eyes at the delicious roughness of being claimed by my first God. I hover over Daddy, rocking violently as Papa chases his orgasm.

"So close," he says, his fingers digging into my hips as he uses me to reach his oblivion. "So good, angel. So fucking good. Fuck, fuck, *fuck!*"

With a primal roar, he snaps his hips, and I actually *feel* him throbbing and spurting deep inside me. I sob and blabber *"Please"* and *"Yes"* over and over again, chanting Daddy's and Papa's names like a prayer.

I'm not sure how long he stays inside me after he's done, but my whole body is thrumming when he finally extracts himself. I'm so desperate to come but also overwhelmed and sore, and I know it's not over yet. I've never run a marathon, but I imagine the physical endurance to be something not too dissimilar.

Papa sighs with bone-deep satisfaction, kissing down my spine, then giving a single lick along my poor, abused hole. I whimper, but Daddy kisses my mouth, swallowing the sound.

"You were so perfect, baby boy," he assures me. "Better than I could have ever dreamed."

Papa flops down beside Daddy before leaning up to kiss me as well. He's slick with sweat, his skin is flushed and his hair is disheveled.

He looks stunning.

I did that to him.

"You felt so fucking incredible, baby boy," he says, shaking his head, his grin so wide it looks like his face might split open. "Thank you for letting me be your first. I'm so fucking honored and shit."

I laugh at his crudeness despite my physical distress. "You were amazing," I say hoarsely. I reach for his hand, and he takes it eagerly, entwining our fingers. "Thank you for being my first."

Daddy reaches up and caresses the side of my face. "Are you ready for Daddy now?"

I look into his eyes and swallow. I'm so tired, but adrenaline shoots through me, and I feel a second wind come over me. "Yes, Daddy," I croak. "Fuck me, Daddy."

In a rare display of losing control, Daddy hisses and bites his lower lip, his eyes smoldering as he looks me up and down. "Ride your Daddy Zeus like he's Pegasus into the clouds," he commands.

I shuffle backward but keep my fingers linked with Papa. I use my other hand to reach behind and find Daddy's cock, angling it into my cum-slick, stretched-out hole. After Papa's monster, Daddy's doesn't feel nearly as bad. In fact, it feels wonderful as I slide all the way down to the root, squeezing my muscles against him. He cries out and grabs my hips. I'm going to have bruises there from both of them.

I can't wait.

"Who's your Daddy?" he growls as I begin to rock.

"You are," I cry back. "Daddy, oh, Daddy!"

He's jackhammering into me already, rock hard from watching me get fucked by Papa. "Say my name, angel. Who am I?"

"Daddy!"

*"Who am I?"*

"Daddy Zeus! Zeus, my God!"

The bed is rocking like crazy. I look down as I bounce on Daddy's dick as he fucks me hard and fast. *"Mine, mine, mine,"* he snarls. My leaking cock jerks like a puppet on a string, but he doesn't touch it.

I have to come last, that's the rule. Daddies come first.

Inside me.

Oh, gods. I really am such a slut, and I *love* it.

"Say my name, baby," he grunts. "Who's gonna come in your pretty ass?"

"Daddy Zeus," I rasp back, my eyes locked with his as he hurtles toward his climax. Papa's big hand grips mine as he watches us with wide eyes.

"So hot," he whispers.

It tips Daddy over the edge. He arches his back and pushes his head into the pillow as I'm filled with hot, thick cum for the second time. I dig the fingers from my free hand into one of his pecs and keep riding him until he relaxes and stills me by stroking my sides.

"Good boy," he mumbles sleepily as I slow to a halt. "So fucking good for your Daddies. Holy shit. Amazing. Perfect. Come here."

He helps ease me off his softening cock, then snuggles me up to his side. He hooks the back of my knee up, so I'm left with an exposed hole again and my hard cock is rubbing against his hairy thigh.

"Papa?" he prompts.

Papa's eyes light up. "Can I?"

They've obviously discussed whatever this is beforehand. Daddy gives him a warm smile and caresses the side of his face. "For a little bit. Baby boy needs to come soon, but you said you'd like it, and you were so fucking spectacular for Daddy. I think you deserve a treat."

They grin at each other before kissing. As wrecked as I am, I still swoon as I watch them. Underneath everything, Daddy is so sweet and thoughtful.

Then I'm squirming and groaning again. Papa moves to bury his face between my cheeks and gently licks out his and Daddy's cum. As good as it feels, my whole body flushes at just how filthy it is, and I paw at Daddy, not sure if I want to get away or not.

Oh, gods. It's *so* hot, though. Dirty but in the best way. So, so intimate.

"Daddy," I whine, tears clinging to my lashes.

He kisses me. "Does that feel nice?" he murmurs.

I pant and squirm, rubbing my erection against him. It does feel good, but my cock *hurts*.

"Yeah, I…uh…oh, Daddy!"

He chuckles fondly before reaching down and running his fingers through Papa's hair. "Our baby needs to come now, Papa. Can you help me?"

I don't want to ruin his fun, but he just grins, his lips shining. "Hell, yeah, Daddy," he enthuses as he bounces back up the bed.

Daddy rolls me onto my back, kissing my mouth and wrapping his hand around my pulsing, sensitive cock. Papa kisses my neck and slips his middle finger inside me. I take it with no problem after everything else. He rubs my taint and fondles my balls. There's enough cum, precum, and lube that Daddy's hand flies easily over my shaft.

I'm screaming into his mouth, clinging to both their chests.

"Come, angel," Daddy commands. "Come for your Gods."

I've never felt anything like it. I explode like a star system coming to life. I have no idea what I say, but I know it's loud and desperate. I claw at my Daddies' skin as I empty and empty until there's not a drop of moisture left inside me. I'm sobbing before I've even stopped spurting, my entire body trembling and convulsing.

And then my Daddies are there, so tightly wrapped on either side of me. Hugging me and telling me I'm beautiful and perfect and safe. They kiss me gently and stroke my limbs as I come back down to earth.

"So good, baby boy. So good."

My heart is still racing as my vision comes back. I blink as I cling to them, feeling their love seep into me as our skin cools.

Because it is love.

I'm not sure if we'll ever be able to speak of it out loud. I don't know if it will last.

But in that moment, I am loved and worshipped. They might be my Gods, but they make me feel like the center of the whole universe.

If I never get a moment like this again, at least I'll be able to treasure this memory forever.

# CHAPTER 14

## Marty

"Sorry! 'Scuse me! Comin' through!"

People practically dive out of my way as I run through the crowded quad. Normally, I'd never charge like this outside of the field. But I have to get to Gabe *now*, and I'm too excited to wait another damned second.

"Thank you kindly!" I holler as I leap over a couple of young ladies who protect their faces with French textbooks.

Some guys start chanting, "Quinn! Quinn! Quinn!" I manage to give them a shaky thumbs up, but I don't break my pace.

I'm on a mission.

Dukey lets me into Alpha Zeta Kappa with a laugh and an eye roll. "Hey, man," he says. "They're upstairs."

I was worried that we were annoying the rest of Seth's house with our increasingly loud fun times. But from what I can tell, they're all quite patiently fond of the situation, so long as we don't keep nobody awake too much. It helps that we're by ourselves on the top floor. The guys know not to go up there, even if we've been all quiet and studying instead of fucking.

Speaking of studying.

"Much obliged!" I cry as I tip my figurative hat at Dukey. I know what figurative means now thanks to Gabe. I'm un-fucking-stoppable.

I take the stairs three at a time, hurtling around Ozo and Tom. "Slow down, big man!" one of them cries. But they're laughing, so I just salute at them.

"Can't, bro!"

I'm out of breath by the time I crash through Seth's door. It occurs to me exactly a second too late that they could have been fucking. We've all agreed it's okay to play between us if someone isn't there, so long as we fill the missing guy in on the fun details afterward. But they're actually sitting at Seth's desk with several textbooks and a bunch of notes.

"Marty?" Daddy says in surprise, clearly thinking something is actually wrong, or he would have called me Papa, then a jackass, then yelled at me to shut the door.

I do that anyway out of habit and lock it before pulling my phone from my pocket and unlocking the screen. "Look!" I say to our boy, feeling my voice catch but actually not giving a damn. I'm so proud I could fucking burst. "Look, baby, look!"

He carefully puts his small hands around mine to steady them as he reads the screen. Then his jaw drops in shock, and I can't help but wiggle in anticipation.

"You got B plus?" he shrieks, looking at me with glassy eyes. "From Professor Knight? A B frigging plus? Papa! You kicked *ass!*"

He throws himself at me, so I haul him up and spin him around. "I've never gotten a B plus in my whole *life!*" I say. "That new TA Professor Knight got this year—Jackson—he's real nice. He sat down with me and talked some stuff through last week. So I felt extra prepared. But really, it's all thanks to you, angel."

I gently place him down and cup my hands on either side of his flushed face. "I'm so proud of you," he whispers, a couple of tears rolling down his cheeks. I kiss them away, then capture his mouth.

"Thank you," I say. But that doesn't seem to be enough, so I kiss him as well, trying to pour everything warm and good that's beating in my heart into him.

I've never felt this way about anyone before. Sure, I want to kiss and fuck him all the time. His skin is like chocolate milk and his mouth like candy. When his mom calls and makes him feel bad, I want to cuddle all the pain away, which I try and do as much as possible. I also want to take the phone off him and give her a piece of my mind, but Daddy promised me that was a bad idea.

I guess what I'm tryna say is that it isn't just physical, although him being a major cutie is never a bad thing. Or the fact that he's so smart and kind he even managed to help this dumb jock get a B fucking plus. He's just…I want to be around him all the time. His happiness is my happiness. He's like sunshine on the beach.

Yeah. I ain't ever felt like this about anyone before, that's for damn sure.

When I break the kiss, baby boy is panting. He looks up at me with swollen lips and flushed cheeks. He *is* a little cherub, and my cock stirs in my shorts. But then Daddy comes up beside me and wraps his arm around my back, tugging at my T-shirt.

"I'm so fucking proud of you as well, big man," he says, his voice low and kind of dangerous. Oh, yeah. My cock definitely bounces in my pants as he seizes my mouth for a filthy kiss. "You deserve a reward. Don't you think, angel? Papa deserves something special?"

Baby boy melts against his side and looks up at both of us

in wonder. "Yes, Daddy," he says sweetly. "Do you want to do that thing we talked about?"

My heart skips in excitement. "What thing?" I ask.

Daddy laughs, but there's nothing mean-spirited about it. In fact, I'd say there was a hell of a lot of affection flowing between us right now.

This is why I've always been drawn to Seth Eisen, and now that I know what he's like as a lover, it's ten times better. Yeah, he's a hard-ass and kinda scary. But it's because he's in charge and knows what's best. When he points that energy at me and our little angel, it's like being inside the best kind of hurricane.

I guess that's what Zeus does, isn't it? He throws lightning bolts, like in a storm.

"Baby boy and I came up with a plan," he says, gripping the back of my neck. "Seeing as he's so good at taking your cock now."

I groan. Our cherub has been stretching with toys and plugs like Coach Drevin stretches us for the damn championships. I was so worried about hurting him his first time, but now he can take me with a much more reasonable amount of prep—by which I mean much quicker, which is good for everyone when we're horny and desperate.

"You wanna fuck, little dude?" I ask hopefully.

He nods and runs his hands over my tummy. My cock jumps again. Seeing him be all confident and shit is such a fucking turn-on. I can't believe this is the same little nerd we met those couple of months ago.

"Yeah, Papa," he says, his voice all sexy. "But not just that."

I look around. "Daddy Z?" I query.

He's still got his hand behind my neck, and he gives me a squeeze. "You fuck baby boy," he explains. "While I fuck you."

My breath catches. "Oh, gods," I moan. "I've wanted you to fuck me for three-and-a-half years."

Daddy chuckles, then pulls me down for another breath-taking kiss. "Too much talk," he growls. "Fewer clothes, now."

I grin at baby boy and wiggle my eyebrows. Then I let them both go and rip my clothes off in record time, making our cherub double up laughing. But Daddy's expression is sizzling. He pulls our angel to him and slips his hand under the hem of his shirt. Baby boy immediately moans and leans against Daddy.

"Doesn't Papa look like a Viking, sweetheart?" he growls into baby boy's ear, loud enough that I can still hear. I puff out my chest and stick my hands on my hips, very much enjoying their hungry looks. "A big, Viking brute all ready to ravage you."

Baby boy makes a sort of pained noise, then yanks off the T-shirt Daddy's been playing with, exposing his slim chest and budded, pink nipples. He's not muscular like Daddy, but he doesn't have the softer layer I do, either. I love that we have three different body types that fit together perfectly.

I bite my lip and run my hand over my thickening cock, picturing just how good this particular combination is going to fit together.

Baby boy lets go of Daddy and runs to me, standing on his tiptoes for a messy kiss. We laugh as we stagger toward the bed, getting rid of his jeans and underwear as we go.

"You're so fucking beautiful," I say as we tumble onto the mattress. It almost sounds like a complaint, I guess, because I still don't really believe that he's mine. How did someone so pretty and smart ever look twice at me?

Well, honestly, I don't care how it happened. Maybe there really are gods watching over us who looked kindly down on me. All I care is that we're here, now, and every time we fuck it's better than the last.

"You're gorgeous," he tells me back, digging his fingers into my shoulders. "And kind and honest and hardworking."

He shakes his head, tears clinging to his lashes again like diamonds, before kissing me like he's afraid I'll disappear.

"Hey, hey, little dude," I say warmly. Like he has to worry about that? Lols. I ain't going nowhere. "It's okay. And thank you. That's real nice to hear you say those things. But I think you see all that because of who you are. Who you make me be. You and Daddy, for sure."

I look over at where Daddy is watching us from the end of the bed. He has his thumbs looped into the belt hooks on his jeans, and he's got a faint, hungry smile on his face. He nods once at me, his gaze simmering through his eyelashes.

Yeah, finally being seen by Seth Eisen is one of the best things to ever happen to me. I can stop tryna make everyone laugh and just be me. If they laugh, that's nice, but I'm not a monkey who has to entertain people to keep myself safe.

I'm just me. Marty Quinn.

Papa.

"I'm so proud of you, Papa," baby boy says again, emotion thick in his voice. "I didn't know the old you, but this you is amazing. Make love to me, please?"

Something catches in my throat. I ain't ever had no one beg me to make love to them before. That's very different from fucking. He wants me to take care of him.

Sometimes during these past few months, it's felt like that I was *born* to take care of him.

I'm just getting silly and in my head and all that, so I smile big and bright and kiss my baby hard. "Of course, darlin'. It would be my pleasure."

He lies on his back and makes the prettiest moans as I stretch him out good and proper with my lubed-up fingers, his ankles wrapped around my back. It's crazy to think that this sweet one was a complete virgin before Daddy and I met him. No kissing or nothing.

Now we're teaching him everything.

"Ahh, you feel real nice, sugar," I say between kisses. "Do you wanna lie like this or on your front?"

"Like this," he says quickly. "I want to see you. To kiss you."

My heart does a little summersault at that. This precious boy.

"Okay, baby. I'd like that, too. So much."

Usually, during sex, Daddy's in charge, and he does all the talking. And that's fine by me. But I like how he's hanging back now and watching as me and baby boy have a moment. Don't get me wrong, he's soon naked and curling up against us, but he stays on the sidelines. He gently rubs my back and occasionally kisses baby boy's cheek, but other than that, he seems so happy to just relax and let us do our thing.

"I'm ready, Papa, please," baby boy begs, making my cock throb and my heart ache. "I can take you. I want you."

I rest our foreheads together for a moment. "Such a good boy," I tell him like I'm saying my prayers at church.

I angle myself between his legs and am about to push my way in when Daddy hands me the bottle of lube with a wink. "Can't hurt," he says, suggesting I should use extra. He's right. We're spending less time on prep, but that should mean more lube.

"Thanks, Daddy," I say, knowing I sound all gooey and shit, but I don't care.

Neither does he. He kisses me, then he gets one of the pillows not under baby boy's head and gets him to lift his hips so it'll be a better angle, or so he says. I never knew that. Damn. I briefly think that I'll need to remember that, but I won't have to. We'll all know that now, won't we?

Feeling all warm and fuzzy, I line myself up again and start pushing my way inside my beautiful baby boy. He bites his lip and takes deep breaths, but he smiles and kisses me, welcoming me inside him.

When I bottom out, we take a moment as always to make sure everyone's okay. Except this time, Daddy places his hand on my lower back.

"Stay there now, big man," he instructs.

I flick my eyebrows as I look down at baby boy, feeling like we're in on a joke together. But then I let out a guttural moan and shiver as Daddy slips a cold, wet finger between my ass cheeks. I feel the mattress dip behind me, then he kisses along my spine and pushes his first finger inside.

I hiss, but I like the burn, and I can tell he knows that.

"Good boy," he says, and I feel those warm fuzzies again.

Yeah, normally, I'm Papa, and I love that. But right now, I'm also his boy, and I love that as well.

"Fuck me, Daddy," I beg. "I'm ready. I want to feel you."

He swats my ass, making both me and baby boy jump. Baby boy looks shocked, but when I break out laughing, so does he.

"Daddy decides when you're ready, naughty boy," Daddy grumbles.

I scrunch up my nose and grin at baby boy. "Oops," I whisper loudly. "Daddy's mad."

He smacks me again on the other cheek, hard. Warmth flows through me and my cock jerks inside baby boy. Oh, fuck, yeah. What is this? I know spanking is a thing but, like, I thought it made you feel bad? I feel *amazing*.

He goes back to fingering me. "You're getting fucked now because baby boy is so good and patient," he continues to grumble. "But sometime very soon I think you need your ass lit on fire. Such a bad boy."

I nuzzle my nose against baby boy's and whimper. He digs his fingers into my arms and kisses the corner of my mouth.

"I don't know what you're talking about," I complain to Daddy.

He slaps the back of my thigh, and I wail in ecstasy. Fuck! This is *awesome!* And he's so *strong* it really does hurt in the most delicious way.

"Bad *boy*," he growls.

I look over my shoulder. "You love it," I say with a grin.

He hums noncommittally, but he does lean over and kiss me filthily. "You okay, baby boy? Papa isn't boring you?"

I bark out a laugh, and baby boy giggles, reaching up to cup the side of my face. "He feels amazing," he says sincerely.

Daddy only had two fingers in my ass, but he yanks them out now. "I think you want it hard and fast," he hisses into my ear.

"Fuck, *yes*, Daddy," I say back, not caring that I sound like a needy slut.

In this house, sluts are worshipped.

I feel him drizzling more lube, and then—*fuck*—he's forcing his cock inside me. I cry out at the sudden burn, but only because of the shock. I love the rough edges and commanding nature. I want to be fucking *taken* by this man.

"Yes, Daddy, *yes*," I utter, shaking as I hold baby boy to me. "Like that. Oh, gods, *yes*."

"Papa," baby boy whispers, cupping his hands on either side of my face as we gaze at each other and kiss. It's not long before Daddy starts fucking me properly, rocking me into baby boy. *"Yessss,"* he hisses, making that face that lets me know I'm hitting his prostate.

And—*ohmyfuckinggods*—Seth Eisen is *in* me. He's fucking me. Just like I always hoped he would for so long. I'd given up hope he'd even notice me, let alone like me, and now we're here, and it's the *best* thing ever!

It doesn't take long to get lost in the sensation. In the rhythm. It's too perfect. Daddy fucks like a goddamn steam train, just like I knew he would. Baby boy squirms and cries beneath me, calling me 'Papa' and telling me I'm amazing, the best, wonderful.

And as I come, feeling baby boy squeeze around me and Daddy blow his load inside me, I decide that my life could do with more B pluses if this is what it gets me.

Love.

I think what this whole thing has gotten me is real, true love. For two men. From my Daddy and my boy.

The gods really did bless me, didn't they?

# CHAPTER 15

## Gabe

By the time I leave the library that night, it's getting late. Darkness has settled and there's a chill in the fall air. Campus feels quiet, but it's not deserted yet, so it doesn't feel creepy.

I take a deep breath and sigh, squeezing the handles on my backpack where they rest on my shoulders. Between all the tutoring and sex marathons, I was starting to fret about my own grades slipping. But my Daddies are at an away game tonight, so I took the time to finish one of my papers and do some proper reading. I feel a lot calmer about everything and like my sense of equilibrium has returned.

I love my life.

Sometimes the dark clouds creep overhead, and I worry what's going to happen afterward. After Daddy and Papa graduate (because they *are* going to graduate. I'd bet not just a thousand dollars but my life on it). I worry what's going to happen after *I* graduate and have to go back home. I've accepted that inheriting the restaurant will be inevitable, at least for now. But I also assume I'll have to go back into the closet.

That's going to be horrendous.

But to be honest, the idea of dating anyone after my Daddies is painful as well. I'm sure it's probably just puppy love talking, but I don't think I'm going to be hopping on Collr or any of those other dating apps anytime soon, looking for a replacement.

Or two. I wouldn't know how to have just one boyfriend or one Daddy now. It's too perfect with the mix of Daddy and Papa. I don't imagine I could get Daddy's red-hot assertiveness or Papa's soul-earnest adoration and goofiness in just one man.

I'm a lucky, lucky boy, and for now, I'm counting my blessings.

I realize too late that I'm daydreaming about my Daddies and not paying attention to my surroundings as I walk away from the library. I can't say I blame myself. I have too many amazing memories rolling around my head now of the times we've spent together. The other evening Daddy was working hard on a paper (which made me super proud anyway), but he insisted that Papa and I stay at Papa's place and have a night just the two of us. It was different without Daddy—still amazing—but also softer and sillier.

I'm too busy recalling how Papa sucked my cock until I came. Usually, I'm the one doing the swallowing, so this was a special treat that I absolutely loved. One second, I'm grinning to myself, thinking about how perfect he made me feel.

The next thing I know, Logan frigging McKenna is stepping out from a little side path and blocking my way.

I stumble to a halt and blink stupidly at him. I shouldn't be afraid. What can he actually do to me? Even if he were capable of something malicious, there are still people milling around in the distance. All I'd have to do would be to scream really loudly to get their attention.

Still, fear tingles down my spine as he smirks and looks

me up and down. I've seen him from afar, but I haven't spoken to him since we made that stupid bet after the Panthers game.

Well, the bit with the money was stupid.

Agreeing to tutor my Daddies was one of the best decisions I've made in my life.

I want to ignore him and walk around him, but that just feels really awkward and rude. Even if he's a terrible person who said awful, hurtful things about my Daddies. I decide to be the bigger person.

"Hello, Logan," I say evenly, gripping my backpack straps. "Can I help you?"

He scoffs and lets his own backpack drop to the ground by his feet. "Oh, I think you've been helping enough. I hear you've been quite the busybody." He looks around, pulling a stupid face like he's perplexed. "Where are dumb and dumber?"

I scowl. "If you're referring to Seth and Marty, they're playing a game out of state. And they're not dumb."

He curls his lips. "You writing their essays for them isn't going to win you that bet, you know. Come May, you're all going to have to pay up."

I feel myself getting upset and almost shout at him. But that's what he wants. So I take a breath, shrug, and smile. "We'll see."

I try and move around him, but he steps in front of me again. My heart skips a beat in a scary way. But I remind myself that there are still plenty of people around. I'm okay.

"If they cheat, it doesn't matter if they get some bit of paper," Logan threatens darkly. "You'll all have to forfeit and pay up. I doubt anyone will want to sign Eisen either if word goes around that he's faking his way through his degree."

I can't help it. I splutter in indignation. "I'm not doing any such thing! They're not cheating! I'm tutoring them, and they're getting better. That's how these things work."

He bites his lip and steps closer to me. I shuffle backward, and he laughs.

"Oh, she works *hard* for the money, so I've heard. Was that always part of the deal from the start?" He steps forward so fast I don't have time to react. Before I know it, he's touching his thumb to my chin. "You help them graduate, and in return, they let you suck their cocks?"

I recoil like I've been burned. "How DARE you," I shout, feeling my cheeks flaming.

He raises his eyebrows and laughs. A couple of people look over, but they keep walking. My pulse is racing, and my hands are trembling.

"Hmm. So…it's not true?" Logan asks in a mocking tone. "You're not a little whore who gets paid in trade? Is it just a status thing, then? You write their essays, and they let you hang out with them." He flicks his eyebrows. "The cock-sucking is just a bonus."

"That's disgusting," I snap. Not the idea of me sucking my Daddies' cocks. I love that. But the notion that it would be part of some sort of paid or barter arrangement.

I love it when Daddy calls me a slut. But only because I'm *his* slut. I am not selling myself sexually for money or popularity or anything so ridiculous like that. My pride is burning, and anger rages inside me.

I know Logan is just a bully and he gets his kicks laughing at other people. But my Daddies mean *everything* to me, and I don't want a reputation like that. He's making it sound dirty in a bad way.

"So, you're *not* sucking their cocks and letting them fuck you every which way till Sunday?" Logan asks in that mock-concerned tone again.

My mouth opens.

Nothing comes out.

I don't want to deny it like it's something to be ashamed of.

"That's a yes, then," he says smugly.

"It's none of your business," I finally snap. There. That's something at least. It's not a denial, but it's not confirming anything, either. "Now, if you don't mind—"

"Oh, but I do," he says with a shark-like grin, stepping closer once again. "What if I want to make it my business?"

I grit my teeth, seeing red. "You might be rich," I spit out. "So that might open doors for you. But you can tell the dean whatever you like. I'm *not* writing either Seth's or Marty's papers, and the truth will out!"

He laughs again, and there's something about it that sends shivers down my spine.

"Oh, no," he says softly, shaking his head and smirking. "I don't care about that, not really. I'm interested in the business of you sucking cock for coin." He gets dangerously close. "How much money would it take for you to suck my cock right now?"

Nausea washes over me, and I really do scream as I shove him away. *"Fuck you, Logan!"* I cry, fighting back tears. "I'd never do that. Not for a *million* dollars. You're obscene!"

"Is there a problem here, gentlemen?"

I spin around to see Ms. Maude folding her arms, wrapping her spider-like fingers around her elbows. A glittering shawl sits on her shoulders, and she stands with the heels of her pointy boots angled together underneath her long, swishy skirt. My chest contracts guiltily, even though she's only looking at Logan.

"N-nothing," I splutter. "We were just talking."

Logan scoffs. "I asked Visoth here a question, and he reacted like a deranged monkey. I have no idea why."

My cheeks burn as hot tears spring into my eyes. But I

clench my fists and try to regain my composure. "I apologize for disturbing the peace," I manage to grit out. I am genuinely humiliated that I've caused a scene. But Logan's revolting proposition has left me wanting to run to the nearest shower and scrub myself raw.

I'm not a whore, am I? Anyway, he's using that word without understanding what it can mean. Ancient Greece had courtesans who were greatly admired. They granted favors and engaged in philosophy themselves. Who's a moron like Logan to judge what they or any sex workers do? I know I don't want people to be gossiping about me, but what would they really be saying?

That I love being with my boyfriends? Ohhh, what a scandal.

No. What I'm horrified by most right now is the idea that he thought he could buy his way into my bed. I'm physically sickened by the notion. He's a terrible person, and I'd never, ever let him touch me.

Ms. Maude's eyes flick between the both of us. "I'd be careful asking questions if you're not prepared for the answers, Mr. McKenna. Your aura is looking particularly green around the edges. That kind of energy is like catnip to karma. If I were you, I'd be watching my back."

He raises his eyebrows. "Did you just *threaten* me?" he splutters. "Anyway, I know all about your witchy mumbo jumbo. It's all made up nonsense. Curse me all you want with your stupid cauldron!"

The corner of Ms. Maude's lips twitch. "Don't be silly, child. There's no such thing as magic." She juts her chin toward him. "When I said watch your back, I meant it literally."

I frown and glance at Logan, only to burst out laughing.

Clayton, the trash panda, has appeared by Logan's backpack. The zipper had been closed when he'd dropped it there a few minutes ago, but now it's fully open. In one hand, Clayton is holding what looks to be half of a peanut butter and jelly sandwich.

The other is holding what has to be Logan's phone.

*"Hey!"* Logan screeches when he realizes what's happening. Clayton is gone in a flash, sprinting into the foliage, still clutching his prizes. Logan snatches up his bag and runs after him, but I don't like his chances.

That little guy can *move.*

A shaky laugh escapes my throat, and I rub my chest as if trying to massage some of the stress away. That was awful, undeniably. But now the moment has passed, I can see that it was just words.

Hateful words, but Logan McKenna has no real power over me.

"You dropped this."

I turn around, slightly startled to discover Ms. Maude right beside me. She's holding out a small burlap bag, not much more than an inch long.

"Oh, no, I don't think so—" I begin to tell her cheerfully.

She takes my hand and presses the bag into my palm. "Don't lose it again," she says firmly. Up close, I can appreciate what an icy blue her eyes are beyond all that eyeliner, and I gulp as she looks unflinchingly at me with them.

"O-okay," I say.

She nods once, then releases me and walks with her head held high back toward the library. Out of nowhere, her nameless black cat appears, entwining around her legs as they both slink inside the building.

I look down at the tiny bag, wondering what's inside it. Then I decide it's probably best if I don't know.

Still, I drop it into one of the small inner pockets of my backpack, figuring it can't harm to keep it on me.

There's still no sign of Logan or Clayton, but I think it's

probably best if I head off anyway. I don't want to run into him again.

The farther I walk, the better I feel. What do I care what stupid, horrible Logan McKenna thinks of me? If he really did want a blow job, he's going to be waiting until the end of days. I'd prefer to pay him the thousand dollars rather than have him anywhere near me.

He's nothing to me.

Especially when I have the most amazing boyfriend Daddy Gods in the entire world. Logan can't hurt me.

Not while I have them.

# CHAPTER 16

## Seth

I THINK I'M ABOUT TO EXPLODE.

That game was a fucking slaughterhouse. It would have been better in front of a home crowd, but a win is a win, no matter what. Besides, now we're one step closer to the championships, and Coach Drevin told me tonight that there are at least two scouts definitely interested in coming to see me soon.

I'm king of the fucking world. I really am a god.

I had half a plan to try and find a way back to Paddle Creek tonight so Marty and I could fuck our little angel senseless. But my car is back at the house as we took the bus with the team, and I figure we can wait until tomorrow to celebrate all three of us.

Besides, by the time I've got a few beers in me and we exit the locker room, I've come up with another scheme that kind of involves all three of us anyway.

"Got any plans, big man?" I mutter into Marty's ear as we push our way out into the night and head toward our hotel. Some of the guys intend to continue the party out in the woods, but I've got something a little more intimate in mind.

It sure is swell being the captain and having the power to assign hotel roommates.

Marty grins at me. "I was thinking of getting an early night, Captain," he says cheerfully. "How 'bout yourself?"

"Early night sounds good," I say, barely containing my simmering lust.

I think I hear a couple of the guys snicker, but I ignore them. I'm sure most of the team has noticed that we're no longer fighting like cats and dogs, and the guys in Alpha Zeta Kappa definitely know something is going on between us. But frankly, I don't give a shit. So long as they still respect me on the field—and as evidenced by our magnificent win tonight, they do—then they can speculate all they want about who and how I'm fucking.

I practically shove Marty through our door when we get to our room, automatically locking it behind us. He grins as I push him toward the bed, eagerly leaning down to meet me for a filthy kiss when I grab his T-shirt and haul him to me.

"You were like a fucking steam train out there," I growl against his mouth, clawing at his chest. "Every time you slammed into one of those suckers, I just wanted it to be me you were plowing."

"Yeah, Daddy?" he asks, already breathless. "You want some of this?"

He grabs himself lewdly. I smack his hand away and seize his jaw. It doesn't stop him from grinning, but I glare at him, the heat blazing between us.

"Naughty boy," I snarl. "That's mine."

I drop to my knees and yank down his shorts. They're the elastic ones he tends to lounge around in, and I spotted in the changing room that he hadn't bothered with any underwear.

It seems I wasn't the only horny fucker after that exhilarating game.

I've never sucked his monster dick before, but it now feels

like the right time. He's oh-so-casually mentioned the idea of topping from the bottom a few times, but I've always pretended like I missed the hint. Not because I want to fight anymore—those days are long gone. But because I'm Daddy, and *I* decide how and when we fuck.

Right now, I want to choke on that beast.

He moans and grips my hair as I get about half of him in my mouth. I don't bother trying to deep-throat him. Right now, the point is just to tease him and get him worked up.

I think it's working.

"Oh, Daddy," he cries, already sounding hoarse and shaky. "Fuck, yes. That's amazing. Oh, gods, your mouth is so good."

I play with him for a little while longer. Then I pop off suddenly and without warning, loving how he winces and gasps.

"On the bed," I command from on my knees. "Clothes off. On your back."

"Make me," he challenges.

I wrap my hand around his cock and squeeze hard. He wails but doesn't try to pull away from me. Instead, he throws off his T-shirt and kicks away his shorts and shoes.

Still gripping tightly to his wet, throbbing member, I rise to my feet, glaring at him.

"Get on the bed, naughty boy."

He pants but still doesn't move, only flicking his eyebrows at me. "Make me, Daddy," he rasps.

I shove his solid chest. If he wanted, he could have stayed completely in place, not moving an inch. Instead, he allows me to topple him backward onto the mattress, and he hurriedly scuttles up the bed like a crab, his eager eyes never leaving me.

I take my time to strip, loving how hungrily he's watching me. I know exactly where I packed our lube, so I fetch it, pumping a little into my palm before I take myself in hand.

Keeping the bottle beside us, I crawl up the bed, hovering over him, my lips inches from his.

"Tell me how you fucked our baby boy the other night," I murmur, licking into his mouth. "Was it sweet?"

He moans and runs his hands up and down my sides. "So sweet, Daddy. Oh, gods, he was so beautiful for me."

"What did you do first?" I ask. He's about to respond, but then he sees me squeeze more lube onto my fingers.

He pauses when he realizes that I'm reaching around to finger *myself.*

"Daddy?" he croaks.

I bite his lower lip savagely, then drag it through my teeth. "Naughty boy. Daddy Zeus asked you a question. Tell your God how you pleasured our precious angel. Did you make him scream?" I glance down. "Touch yourself, big man. Keep that monster cock rock hard for me."

His breathing is ragged, and his brown eyes are wide, but he gets some lube and starts to jerk himself off leisurely.

"I-I undressed him," he begins to tell me. "Slowly. He giggled a lot. He was real fucking cute, Daddy. I kissed him all over. Then when he was naked, I gently laid him down and gave him the best ever blow job. That was slow, too. I think he liked being teased. He needed a bit of time to recover after he came down my throat, so I turned him over like a little piggy on a spit. I got naked, too, and then took my time eating him out. His ass is like a fucking *peach*, Daddy."

I groan, adding a second finger to my own ass. "So sweet and juicy," I agree. "You look so hot when you lick him clean. Did he squeal and squirm?"

"Yeah, yeah," Marty says, my naughty, slutty God boy. "He makes the most delicious noises, Daddy. I told him he was good and sweet and perfect, just like you do. He was almost crying by the time I was ready to fuck him. But the good crying, y'know?"

"I do," I murmur. "He's so pretty when he begs, so desperate for your huge cock. How did you fuck him?"

"Lotsa ways," he says, closing his eyes for a moment and sighing. "On his hands and knees. On his back. But then we cuddled. I sat up against the pillows, and he straddled my lap, bouncing on my big dick, crying while I jerked him off all slow and sweet."

"Urgh," I utter, capturing his mouth for a rough kiss. "Did you eat your cum out of his ass?"

"After I licked all his off his tight little body," he says. "It's like salted caramel ice cream."

"You're such a fucking cum slut," I growl, forcing a third finger inside myself. "I love watching you eat up all our spunk. My own filthy fucking caveman."

"I thought I was your Viking, Daddy?" he asks playfully.

I yank his leg up and smack his thigh with my clean, free hand. "You're whatever I tell you to be, naughty boy. Caveman. Viking. Gladiator. It doesn't matter. What matters is you're *my* big, dirty slut, and I get to fuck you whenever and however I want."

He grins. "One day, Daddy, will you spank me until I come? I want you to make my ass red and so sore I ain't gonna be able to sit for a week."

I kiss him messily. "One day, naughty boy. I'll have you begging for my hand. Maybe we can get you one of those paddles with the Alpha Zeta Kappa letters cut into it. Really make that big ass shine and remind you who you belong to."

He makes a desperate sound that lets me know the research I've been doing into that kind of BDSM hasn't been wasted.

"Shall we make baby boy watch when I spank your ass?"

"Maybe I could suck his cock?" he asks hopefully, and I have to laugh at how sweet my big man can be when talking about such debauched things.

"Sounds heavenly, naughty boy," I tell him. "But not today. Today, Daddy is going to ride your monster cock and come all over you. Like Theseus defeating the Minotaur."

He groans and digs his fingers into my sides. "I'll be your Minotaur, Daddy. Tame me with your gorgeous hole. Then we can tell our angel all about it afterward."

I smirk. "Oh, I think we can do a little better than that," I tell him playfully.

# CHAPTER 17

## Gabe

For once, I'm almost missing the noisy distraction of my roommate. My room is too quiet, and my thoughts are too loud. The encounter with Logan is troubling me, and I'm torn between telling my Daddies about it or not.

On the one hand, I don't ever want to keep secrets from them. I haven't had to before. I just tell them whatever pops into my head and am constantly amazed that they want to hear it.

On the other hand, I really don't want them to know it even happened. It was horrible, and even after a long shower, I still feel icky. I can't actually believe Logan said that to me. He can't have really meant it, can he? I don't think he's interested in men anyway. Even if he's one of those people who just sees a cock-sucker as a mouth and gender doesn't matter, why would he want *me?* He could easily go to Creams if he felt like trying it with a guy, not to mention that he's got plenty of girls interested in him—thanks more to his money than his personality, I'm sure.

I chew on my thumbnail. I just wish it hadn't happened. I

guess I'm a bit scared that if my Daddies think other people see me as some kind of common whore, they won't want me anymore. I know I'm *not* that, but my brain is going down an illogical spiral.

I only have a precious few more weeks with them before we break for Christmas (and Hanukka for Seth). After that, who knows what's going to happen. I don't want to risk everything falling apart now.

It's not helping that I haven't heard from them since the game. A quick internet search told me that they won, so I assume that they're out celebrating or something—and that's awesome. Of course they should be happy, and not everything revolves around me. But it's unlike them not to check in.

I try and shut my stupid brain up by watching some silly TikToks, but I practically fall out of bed when a notification comes up in our group chat. Not long after we got together, Papa changed the name from 'Study Buddies' to 'Heaven,' and it makes me smile every time I see it. The chat icon is a photo we took of them both kissing my cheeks, and I'm laughing with my eyes shut and my nose scrunched up.

It makes my heart warm without fail to look at it now. I'm so silly to be worrying. Everything's fine. Of course my Daddies haven't forgotten about me, and they probably don't need to know anything about Logan's horrible request.

I shake off my previous melancholy and turn my attention to the message. It's a video, which piques my curiosity. Maybe it's my Daddies sending me a drunken goodnight message. I eagerly exit the other app and open up our chat.

It takes more than a minute to download, which has me wondering how long it is.

Then I see the preview image, and my heart stops.

Before daring to click on it, I run over to my door and

lock it. My roommate said he wouldn't be back until well after midnight, and he's got his key if he does need to get back in.

But I have a strong feeling I don't want to be interrupted anytime soon.

I rush back to lie on my bed. My heart in my mouth and my lower lip between my teeth, I tap on the play icon, holding my breath.

The video preview wasn't lying to me. Daddy is straddling Papa, and they're both totally naked. I can see Daddy is hard, but I'm not sure about Papa because it looks like his cock is *inside Daddy.*

Daddy leans back, presumably from where he just hit the record button on his phone. It's positioned just behind Papa's left shoulder, but he's still able to look over and grin at the screen as well. Daddy runs his hand down his chest and licks his lips.

"Hey, baby boy," he says, and my heart aches. You'd think I hadn't seen them in weeks instead of just yesterday. "Your Daddies miss you. We thought you'd like to see what we got up to after the game." He strokes his straining cock and rolls his hips, making Papa moan wantonly. "Tell our angel what we've been up to, naughty boy."

Papa lets out a weak chuckle like he's being tortured, and if Daddy is making him wait to fuck him, I'm sure that's exactly what he feels like.

"Daddy sucked my cock, baby boy," he says hoarsely, reaching up and pinching both of Daddy's nipples between his fingers and thumbs. "Then he pushed me onto the bed, made me jerk off while he fingered himself, and now he's going to ride my brains out like a bucking bronco."

Daddy's grin is wolfish. He leans down and kisses Papa, rocking his hips again and still leisurely stroking his cock.

Good *gods,* I'm already so hard, but I'm so mesmerized by the video I don't dare tear my gaze away.

Daddy knocks Papa's hands down, then pins them over his head as he starts to undulate faster against his hips, impaling himself harder and deeper on Papa's giant cock. "You like that, big man?" he rasps.

"You feel fucking amazing, Daddy," Papa cries. "So tight, so good."

"My Minotaur," Daddy growls, and I know it's not that important right now, but the fact that he's come up with a classical sexy nickname for Papa is *so hot.* I'm panting as I watch them fuck hard and fast.

The camera must be on the nightstand or something because the hotel bed is rocking and shaking like crazy, but the video is steady, thank the gods. I don't want to miss a second of this. Papa is wailing and grunting, thrusting his hips up over and over again to slam against Daddy's prostate. Daddy is dripping with sweat as he continues to hold Papa's hands over his head and ride him hard.

"That's it, naughty boy. You fuck Daddy's ass like the huge slut you are. Come for me, big man. Empty that enormous cock and give Daddy all your cum."

As he climaxes, Papa's wails turn into a bellow so loud it has me glancing at the door, hoping no one is walking past. But so what if they are? My Daddies have made a frigging *porno* for me, and it's one of the hottest things I've ever seen. If anyone hears, they can just be jealous.

Daddy keeps thrusting until he's wrung Papa out. I can tell because Papa's whole large body goes limp. Daddy lets go of his wrists to cup either side of his face and kiss him passionately. I quiver, drinking it all in like I need to commit it to memory. I can't believe I'll be able to watch this whenever I want. It doesn't seem fair to the rest of the world, and yet I know I'll never share it with anyone else as long as I live. This is my special gift from my Daddies.

"Good boy," Daddy murmurs, nipping at Papa's mouth. "You fucked me so hard. Now you just relax while Daddy paints you."

"Yes, Daddy," Papa says sleepily. He paws at the side of Daddy's jaw before letting his arm drop. I can only see his profile, but I can tell that he's looking up at Daddy in adoration.

I know the feeling.

I barely breathe as Daddy's hand flies over his red, straining cock. He looks utterly magnificent as he brings himself to the edge, Papa's cock still inside him. Then suddenly, he's coming everywhere, spraying Papa's chest and face like a can of whipped cream. He takes his time to milk out the last drop, then grins and sucks on his index finger before looking back into the camera. I jump, even though that's so silly. They made the video *for* me. But I can't help but feel like I've been caught snooping.

Daddy smiles at the screen, though. "We hope you loved that, baby boy," he says seductively. Then he leans forward and stops the video with his clean finger.

My breaths seem *really* loud all of a sudden in the silence. I'm shaking and hard and sweating. Without thinking, I rip off my pajamas and fumble with my own camera.

I have to jerk off *right now.*

So why can't I send a video back?

My heart is hammering in my chest as I position myself just right. I don't think because I know I'll talk myself out of it. Instead, I marvel at the fact that I've gone from shy virgin to the boy with a camera pointed at his cock and hole, then press record.

"Um, hi, Daddies," I say breathlessly, fondling my dick. "I

loved your video so, *so* much. I thought I'd show you how much."

I keep my eyes closed throughout most of it as I don't want to risk watching what I'm doing and changing my mind. But I moan as I start jerking off. When I have enough precum, I scoop it off the tip of my cock with my other hand, then start fingering my hole.

"Daddy," I whisper. "Papa. Oh, *oh*."

I was so ridiculously turned on when I started it doesn't take me more than a minute to come all over my hand and chest. I gasp for air as the room stops spinning. Then I think of Papa and lick some of my mess off my fingers.

"Night, night, Daddies," I say sweetly, then press stop.

I can't believe I just did that.

I don't even watch it back other than the first and last couple of seconds to make sure it filmed okay. I upload it to the chat, then grab a towel to rush out to the communal bathroom to have a shower before my housemate can come back and see the state I'm in.

Being under the hot water means I can't anxiously check the chat for replies. Instead, I let my hands roam over my still-tingling skin, feeling no small amount of awe at myself.

I made a sex tape.

I'm a rock star.

I giggle to myself as I get out and dry off. Obviously, I wouldn't do it for anyone else on the planet other than Daddy and Papa, but the fact that they care for me so much I've got the confidence to do it is astounding.

I feel unstoppable. Like I could climb Mount Olympus.

By the time I finally do check my phone, Daddy and Papa have both replied.

PAPA: OMG LITTLE DUDE!! YOU'RE SO HOT AND SEXY!!! LOVE LOVE LOVE IT!!!!

DADDY: Daddy's proud of you, little angel. So perfect for your Daddies. Sleep well and we'll cuddle you tomorrow.

He's also sent a photo of them snuggled up in bed that makes my heart melt. I hug my phone to my chest.

Screw Logan McKenna. My life is perfect, and there's *nothing* he can do to change that.

# CHAPTER 18
## *Marty*

*"TOUCHDOWN!"*

I look over as the clock flicks to zero, and release a feral kind of roar along with the rest of my teammates. We all rush the field to where Daddy is holding the ball aloft that he just slammed into the ground.

It's not that we won another game—although that's pretty dang awesome. It's that there are no less than *three* scouts here who came to watch my Daddy play, and he couldn't have given them anything more. He's a fucking star, and I'm just all filled up with love for him.

I haven't said that out loud, of course. Because he hasn't said it. The L-word, I mean. But I ain't ever felt like this about anybody before, and I know that I love both Daddy and our angel boy. In different ways, sure, but that kinda makes it better. I get to have *two* kinds of love.

What a lucky sonofabitch I am.

I'm not the first to reach Daddy, but I push my way through the guys so I can be the one to duck down and lift him onto my shoulders. The home crowd is going crazy, and even though I can't see him, I know baby boy is out there cheering his heart out.

It took a while to convince him that it was okay to come to our games. I think he's still a little worried that we don't want to be seen with him. Which is crazy, but at least now he comes along. I feel like he's our lucky charm.

How nuts is it that Daddy and I found ourselves an adorable nerd boyfriend who *also* likes football? The more I think on it, the more I reckon he really was sent down to us from heaven by the gods.

The team waves to the screaming crowd as the Paddle Creek Kittens perform a victory cheer routine, waving their pom-poms and doing backflips. We've still got the semifinals to get through before the championships in January, but that doesn't make this victory feel any less sweet. In fact, it's a damn fine way to end the year. I bounce Daddy on my shoulders as he beats his chest and roars back at the stands.

*"Eisen! Eisen!"* they're chanting.

I'm so proud of him I'm just about fit to burst. Damn, I love this game so much.

Sometimes I worry who I'll be when I'm not a Panther anymore, but I figure Daddy and baby boy will help me figure it out.

As long as I have them, I know I'll be all right.

Eventually, Daddy taps my shoulder, and I let him down. He grips my arm and beams at me. "Big man," is all he says in an emotional rasp.

I clap him on the back and glance to where those scout guys are talking with Coach Drevin. I don't know what they're saying, but after that game, I'm real sure it's gotta be positive.

"You did good, Captain," I tell Daddy back. I want to call him Daddy and kiss the shit outta him, but I can do that later.

Sometimes I think it's even better to be happier for

someone else than yourself. I feel like I'm watching his dreams come true right before my eyes.

He deserves it. He's worked so damn hard both on and off the field. He might seem scary, but he's really one of the kindest guys I've ever met.

Gods, I can't wait to introduce him and baby boy to my momma. Maybe we can take a road trip over the summer once we've graduated. We'd all fit in my crappy car, I'm sure. Though I guess it depends where Daddy gets signed. He might have to drive himself…

I shake my head and watch him moving between the rest of the team, clapping backs and ruffling hair. I'm getting ahead of myself, but it's hard not to feel excited.

I was so hyped to get my free ride into college that I never really stopped to think about what my life might look like afterward. Then my grades went to shit, and I figured what did it even matter?

That was before a certain gorgeous little cherub came into my and Daddy's lives.

As if on cue, I happen to glance up into the stands as we're walking back to the tunnel and spy Gabe watching me. He immediately lights up and waves like crazy, making me laugh. Gods, I can't wait to hug him and spin him around. I want to kiss him and scream from the rooftops that he and Daddy are all mine.

So far, we haven't precisely hidden our relationship, but it's not exactly public yet, either. Maybe after Christmas, things will change. Daddy will know if he's been signed when we come back in spring. He's mentioned a couple of times that he's not going to let anyone put him back into the closet, so if he's going to tell his new team about our rela-tionship, surely we can tell Paddle Creek? The thought makes me feel even more awesome than winning the game.

Unfortunately, not everything's swell.

I catch McKenna's eye just before I head into the tunnel to go to the locker room. His face has an expression I can't quite read, but whatever. I'm unsurprised he's not cheering for Daddy, but you'd at least think he'd be a bit happy, seeing as his buddy Perkins is on the team as well.

Some people are just miserable, I guess. Anyway, it sucks to be him. If we carry on the way we are, me and Seth are totally gonna graduate, and then he'll be out three large ones.

I forget about him and continue celebrating with all my teammates. I like that guys like Dukey from Alpha Zeta Kappa are more friendly with me now. I'm glad we'll have next semester at least to keep being buddies. A lot of the guys will still be here next year as well, so maybe after graduation, me and Daddy can come back and catch a game or two. We'll be visiting baby boy a lot, no doubt, so we'll be around anyway.

I shower quickly. I want to be squeaky clean for Daddy and baby boy, but if we celebrate the way I think we're probably gonna, I'm sure another shower will be in my near future.

Worth it for all the mind-blowing orgasms, to be honest.

There are gonna be fans outside wanting photos and videos and stuff with the team. I'm not people's first choice, but Daddy is. I throw on my jeans as well as a T-shirt and button-down so I'll look nice for Daddy just in case we get any photos together. I feel like I've done the town proud tonight, and Momma always says it doesn't hurt to look the part. I even spritz a little aftershave. Baby boy says he likes it when I smell like a real Viking, but sometimes it's nice to be all flowery and shit.

Seth looks fucking gorgeous, even though he's just in his letter jacket and jeans. He's glowing from running his ass off on the field, and his hair is shiny after showering. I bump shoulders with him as we walk out together into the cold

November air, grinning and hoping my dumb face says all the things I want to tell him out loud.

I'll tell him later. With my words, but also with my mouth and other body parts.

Aw, yeah. I can't wait.

Outside of the stadium, a blur rushes toward us, and in a flash there's a little angel with his arms wrapped around us both.

I laugh and rub his back as Daddy kisses the woolen hat on top of his head.

"Hey, cherub," he says quietly as people filter around us.

"You were amazing," baby boy gushes, also keeping his voice low. "I bet all the teams will be fighting over you. Oh, gods, Daddy. You're going to be a star!"

"He is," I say, feeling like my chest expands like a balloon.

Daddy ruffles my hair. "You kicked ass as well, big man."

"Of course!" baby boy agrees.

But I shake my head and smile. "Not like you, Captain. This is *your* moment. I'm just tickled pink to be a part of it."

"Well, isn't this cute?" a horribly familiar voice drawls, spoiling the mood immediately.

My head snaps up as I release my guys. I scowl at McKenna. "Can we *help* you?" I say, not too politely.

I'm not pleased to see him, but when I glance down to see baby boy's face has gone all pale and he looks like he's gonna barf, I really do feel like a caveman or a Viking. I pull him against my side and scowl twice as hard as McKenna approaches. I'm not sure what exactly has gotten my angel so spooked, but I ain't having none of it. It's probably just McKenna's stupid face, but there's a little voice in my head saying it's something more.

"Let's go, please," baby boy hisses.

"Gabe?" Daddy says.

It's kinda amazing how in one word, he can feel like he's

suddenly radiating like a nuclear power plant. He snaps his head toward McKenna and curls his lip. "Fuck off," he snarls. "Graduation isn't for another six months. Until then, we've got nothing to say to you, rich boy."

McKenna scoffs, and I hug baby boy tighter to me, feeling him tremble. Well, shit. Remembering how he was so brave the last time we were all standing outside this stadium, I'm even more sure something hinky is going on.

"Oh, I have *plenty* to say, Eisen," McKenna says with a shrug. "You might not want to hear it, being a pussy-whipped bitch and all."

I feel anger rise in me like a bull, but Daddy just grits his teeth. I feed off his energy and calm the fuck down. People are staring. It's not like last time when we made that stupid bet and were mostly alone. There are all kinds of folks stopping and staring.

"Talk all you like. No one's listening," Daddy says, keeping his voice steady. "We're going to celebrate. In case you didn't hear, we won." His smile is tight. "I'm sorry Perkins didn't get to play quarterback, after all. I guess there are some things money can't buy."

"Oh, but there is plenty it can," McKenna fires back, his grin like a shark. "Or did your little slut not tell you he sucked me off for a twenty behind the library?"

My blood runs cold, but before I can get my mouth to engage, baby boy goes off like a firecracker on the Fourth of July.

"*The hell I did!*" he yells, making even more people stop and stare. "You asked me, and I told you to fuck off! You're disgusting, Logan. I wouldn't touch you if you were the last man on earth! Seth, Marty, you've got to believe me!"

"Hey, hey," Daddy says urgently. "Of course we believe you, baby."

"Without a doubt," I cry, hugging him tighter. Our angel would never do anything like that.

"Leave now," Daddy says to McKenna, his voice dangerously low.

McKenna just shrugs all casual-like, though. "I wanted to see what the fuss was about. I was going to offer him a fifty, but it really wasn't that good. Apparently, whoring yourself out to the two of you doesn't *actually* give you any skills."

My arm is raised and my fist curled before I even know what's come over me. How *dare* he talk about our beautiful angel like that? But Daddy grabs me, and I immediately respond to his touch.

"No," he says firmly, his eyes blazing into mine. "You are so much better than that, Marty. He's a pathetic liar, not worth a second of your time."

"I didn't, Daddy, I promise!" baby boy shrieks in absolute panic. He's clinging to me and Daddy now, looking like he's gonna hurl. "I should have told you. I'm sorry. But it was so awful. He said the meanest things to me, but I told him no, I swear!"

McKenna splutters, looking like he's just won the lottery. *"Daddy?"* he repeats incredulously.

Daddy ignores him, and so do I. "Shh, shh," I say to our angel, trying to get him to calm down. "Of course you said no. It's okay, darlin'."

"Oh, you're going to believe that little slut over me?" McKenna scoffs, throwing up his hands. "Who cares. It's obvious you're sharing him and twisting his mind. *Daddy?* I wonder what diseases you're passing between you. Unless…" He covers his mouth and pretends to act shocked. "Are you two fucking as well? Is it like some depraved orgy?"

"Hey!" Dukey shouts. "Cool it, man. Nobody asked you to get all up in their business."

Gods, there are so many people still watching us. Some of

them even still have popcorn from the game. Poor baby boy. Daddy and I can shake this off, but he looks like he wants to die of humiliation.

"Shut it, McKenna," I holler. "No one wants to hear your lies."

"I'm sure plenty of people want to know their beloved captain is secretly a filthy pervert," McKenna sneers back. "Those big-time scouts, for one thing."

*"Fuck you, you jealous little prick!"* I properly shout, startling even myself. I don't ever lose my temper on account of my size. I don't ever want no one feeling unsafe around me. But this little shit has got me hulking out. He's threatening both the men I love, and I won't stand for it.

McKenna just shrugs again, though, like that's all he can do now. "Who cares?" he says like he didn't start this whole thing. "The truth will out, won't it, Visoth?"

It feels like those words have some meaning that I don't quite catch. But I don't get no time to dwell on it.

"Gabriel?" a voice cuts through the murmuring crowd.

Baby boy goes so limp in my arms I fear for a second he's passed out. But he hasn't.

Not yet, at least.

The woman's voice is louder this time. "Gabriel?"

"Mama?" baby boy croaks back.

My head snaps to lock eyes with Daddy.

*"Mama?"* we both repeat.

# CHAPTER 19

## *Gabe*

THIS CAN'T BE HAPPENING.

This *cannot be happening.*

My mother's frightened face emerges from the crowd—whether I believe it or not—like a specter in a dream. She's clutching her car keys to her chest like they might protect her from whatever she's so afraid of.

Me, probably. If she heard any of Logan's cruel words, all her nightmares about me are coming true right in front of her.

Panic floods me, and tears sting my eyes. Instinct tells me to push my Daddies away, but my heart has me clinging on to them harder than ever. *Don't leave me,* I beg silently.

They really are my Gods, though, because they apparently hear my prayer and tighten their grips on me.

"Mrs. Visoth?" Daddy asks with raised eyebrows.

Mama presses her lips together and advances toward us like we're a bomb about to go off. "Gabriel?" she just repeats, disregarding Daddy completely. "What's the meaning of this? What did your friend say about you? Who are these men?"

I can't help the wretched laugh that barks out of my throat. "Logan isn't my *friend,* Mama. He *hates* me."

She bristles, completely ignoring the hundreds of people goggling over this whole exchange. I am acutely aware of them, however. All my secrets are being laid out for the entirety of Paddle Creek to see. I feel like a frog being dissected in a science class.

Except I'm still very much alive.

"He seems to be the only one looking out for you!" she cries. "What kind of a reputation are you giving our family here? We should never have let you leave home. When your resident advisor called to tell me you were in trouble—"

"I'm not in trouble!" I splutter indignantly.

"What do you call this, then?" she demands.

"Drama," Daddy says, his voice like ice. I glance up at him, terrified for a second that he's mad at me. But he's glaring at Logan, and I allow myself to breathe again. "You did this," he snaps. "All of this. You snooped around on my grades, you tried to assault my boyfriend, and I'll bet my entire football career you bribed the RA to have them call Gabe's mom."

"It's Gabriel," Mama snipes, making me cringe. "And what do you mean 'boyfriend'? That's disgusting! Gabriel, you come here to me right now."

"No," I say.

It's quiet, but I say it.

She blinks at me, fury building on her face, and yet I stand firm.

Because—you see—Seth Eisen just told the whole town that *I'm his boyfriend* and I think that means I have the courage to do just about anything now.

"No?" she splutters. "How *dare* you speak to your mother like that. Thank *god* no one from back home can see you like this. Disturbed and disrespectful. Come on. We're leaving immediately. We'll pack up your room and be home before dinner tomorrow. We can pretend this entire misadventure never happened!"

My knees really do give out at that. But Daddy and Papa are still holding on strong, so I don't fall.

"I'm not leaving," I say in horror.

"That's right," Papa chimes in confidently. "Gabe belongs here!"

She scoffs and curls her lip. It doesn't matter how much expensive make-up she has on or how perfect her blonde beehive hair is.

I can see now what an ugly person she is.

"In this rundown town? With perverted men like you? Don't make me laugh. I knew this was a mistake from the start. Come *on*, Gabriel. We're going back where there are good, Christian people!"

I open my mouth, but I don't know what to say.

But someone else speaks for me.

"Something doesn't need to be shiny and new for it to be good," Ms. Maude says, stepping out from the sea of people.

"Ms. Maude?" Ozo from Daddy's house squeaks. "What are you doing here?"

The corner of her lip twitches in the closest thing I've seen to a smile from our faithful librarian. "Oh, I never miss a game, child."

She's dressed all in black in a sea of purple and teal, yet somehow, I believe her.

"And that's not very cool calling the captain those names, ma'am," Dukey says with a frown. "He's a damn fine quarterback, and it's clear he loves your son a lot."

"I do," Daddy says, and my jaw drops open. I feel my eyes go wide as I turn to look at him. But he's staring straight at my mother. "I love both Gabe Visoth and Marty Quinn very much." He squeezes us tightly, and I think I really might pass out this time. "They're both mine."

A cheerleader with dark hair and teal glitter on her eyelids clasps her pom-poms in front of her chest and sighs dramatically. One of the Panthers snaps at another, who produces a fifty-dollar bill without question. Some of the bystanders start filming and taking photos, whispering things like "Holy fuck, of *course* Eisen has *two* boyfriends."

But any warmth I might have felt at their support—or more to the point, Daddy's very public declaration—is extinguished by my mother's disgust and fury.

"How *dare* you, Gabriel," she says, her nostrils flaring. "I thought you were a good boy! Where is your respect? For yourself? For me? For your father? The way you're letting that man touch you…talk about you…" She physically shivers, showing her revulsion.

I lose the battle with my tears as my throat clenches and my stomach turns. "I'm sorry, Mama," I whisper.

"Don't you even *think* about apologizing, baby," Daddy snaps. He cups my face to make me look at him, and even though he's furious, I see the love in his eyes. I want to cling to it like a life raft. "This woman abuses and bullies you. She tries to control you even from hundreds of miles away. She tears you down and tells you that you are nothing and your dreams don't matter. But you are one of the best people I have ever met. You are strong and smart and going to have an amazing life." He pauses and meets the eyes of my horrified mother. "And she needs to decide right now if she wants to keep being a part of it because you don't need her, baby boy. You have us."

"Yeah!" Papa yells, squeezing me so hard he practically lifts me off the ground. "And we love the *shit* out of you, little dude. Now and forever!"

"Don't be ridiculous," Mama says with a nasty laugh. "He's not going to choose you perverts over his own family. You've just…" She waves her hand. "Cast some kind of a spell over him."

"I can assure you they haven't," Ms. Maude mutters.

For a moment, Mama looks between me and my Daddies. "Fine," she suddenly snaps. "If it's a choice, so be it. What will it be, Gabriel? A life of sin that will damn you for eternity? Or forgiveness back where you belong, at home, living with a good, honest woman and supporting your family."

Daddy scoffs. "That's not even a choice, ma'am," he says with a laugh.

"Real classy, Eisen," Logan drawls. My gods, I'd forgotten he was even here. "Breaking up a family now, are you?"

"Give it up, McKenna," my Daddy replies, not even looking at him. "Your daddy doesn't love you. He just writes you checks in between bribing congressmen and fucking the nanny."

A collective gasp goes up through the crowd. "Oh, snap," whispers the teal-glitter cheerleader.

"Mama?" I manage to utter.

She's not serious, is she? She's not making me choose between being who I am and my family. "I'm still me. You don't have to do this."

Her laugh is cold and brutal. "My son would never disrespect me like this. My son is not a perverted *monster.* You can come home right now and live by my rules, or you can never come home at all. No Christmas, no nothing."

My heart lurches. "You're kicking me out?" I whimper. We break for the holidays in only a couple of weeks. What the hell am I going to do?

"Mrs. Visoth—ma'am," Daddy says imploringly. "Don't do this. Gabe is an amazing young man, and we love him very much. There's nothing to punish him for."

She doesn't even look at him or acknowledge him in any way. She's just glaring daggers at me.

"Fuck it," Papa says suddenly very loudly.

The tension between me and my mother appears to snap, at least for me, anyway. I look up to see my Papa smiling. I don't really know why he's cheerful all of a sudden, but love and warmth fill my heart, and I feel like everything's going to be okay.

"You don't want him for Christmas?" Papa says. "We'll have him. Ain't nobody throw down a Christmas turkey like the Quinns. My momma will love the shit outta him." His face suddenly drops, and he looks at Daddy. "Oh, crap. But what about your family?"

The expression that overcomes Daddy's face is a beautiful mixture of fond patience and true love. He squeezes Papa's shoulder and sighs.

"Still Jewish, big man."

There's a second's pause before Papa lets go of us with one arm to punch the air.

"Hell, yeah! Hanukka with the Eisens and Christmas with the Quinns!"

"And New Year's by ourselves," I say, my voice dispassionate sounding despite the storm raging within me. "Mama, don't make me do this. There's nothing wrong with me."

"Or us," Daddy says firmly.

"Throuple goals!" someone shouts from the crowd.

"I love you and Tata," I tell her. "But this is who I am. I'm gay. I love it here in Paddle Creek. And…and I don't want the restaurant. That's your dream, not mine."

"Ungrateful, selfish child!" she shrieks. I have a feeling the confession about the restaurant might have been the thing to break her. At least she might finally be realizing that this is a battle she's not going to win. "After everything your father and I have done for you! Sacrificed for you!"

"And I'm so grateful for that. I really am," I say, begging

her to see sense. "But that doesn't mean you can control my life. You don't own me!"

"No, I love you," she says, sticking her nose in the air. "But you clearly don't love me. Goodbye, Gabriel. You can call me if you find your morality again. Otherwise, don't bother."

Sickness swoops through me as she turns her back on me and starts walking away. I'm shaking, but I won't let her have the last word.

"I choose happiness!" I call after her. "I choose love! I hope you do, too. Goodbye, Mama."

She pauses, and for a second, hope flickers, and I think she might change her mind. But then she keeps walking, her car keys held up like claws, ready to attack anyone who might come near her.

I've been disowned.

There's a roaring, whooshing sound in my ears, and my vision is tilting. I can't feel my legs. But then a voice cuts through everything, bringing me back down to earth.

"Gabe," the black-haired cheerleader says loudly, raising her teal-and-purple pom-poms. She hits them together, rustling them as she shouts my name again. "Gabe. Gabe! GABE!"

I blink as several of her teammates start joining in. Dukey raises his fist in time to the sky.

*"GABE! GABE! GABE!"*

Other bystanders add their voices to the growing chant. I see that Jackson Riggs—Professor Knight's TA—has a purple foam finger that he's waving above the crowd. Somewhere, the marching band begins to bang their drums. Ms. Maude claps demurely, the twitch of her mouth almost a triumphant smirk.

Logan clenches his jaw before vanishing into the throng.

*"GABE! GABE! GABE!"*

I look up in confusion at my Daddies, my mother truly

lost beyond the crowd, perhaps forever. But all I see is them. They're beaming down at me as they hold on to me tight.

"What's happening?" I whisper.

Daddy shakes his head. "You don't need a family that doesn't love or respect you," he says, his voice surprisingly tight. "You already have a family right here that adores you. You're home, and your real life is just getting going."

I look around as the chant becomes a cheer, and I just catch a fleeting glimpse of my mother's car driving off. On top of a dumpster, just visible in the street light, is Clayton, the trash panda. Maybe I'm delirious, but I swear he gives the retreating vehicle a wave.

That's it, then. The end.

Or…is Daddy right? Is this the beginning?

"I love you, Daddy," I whisper, not bothering to fight the tears. "I love you, Papa. Meeting you was the best thing that's ever happened to me."

Papa grins and rubs his face. I realize he's also crying.

Of course he is.

"I think you mean that *you're* the best thing to ever happen to *us,* little dude," he says proudly.

"Damn right," Daddy growls. He closes the hug so we're all facing each other, shutting out the rest of the world for just a second. "Your Papa is a smart guy."

"He is," I say as earnestly as I possibly can. "You both are. My clever Daddy Gods."

"Our perfect angel," Daddy says with a contented sigh. "Come on. Enough drama for one night. Let's go home."

"Home," I repeat fondly.

Home is wherever they are.

# CHAPTER 20

## Seth

WHAT A DAY.

The house is still and empty as my boys and I push our way through the front door. Everyone else is still out celebrating. Besides, I got the feeling they maybe wanted to give the three of us some space.

Baby boy was quiet on the drive home from the stadium. Seeing how supportive the town was toward him and us definitely lifted his spirits, but I think the reality of his situation is sinking in, and my heart wants to break for him.

How could a mother do that to her own child?

Wordlessly, I steer both my boys into the kitchen and fix us all a glass of water and grab some protein bars. Big man wolfs two down as we sit at the kitchen table, but baby boy hardly nibbles his at all. At least he drinks the water, then I pull him to me.

"Come here," I urge him as he straddles my lap, pressing his chest to mine. I kiss his cheek, then rest his head against my neck, hugging him to me and carding my fingers through his hair. Big man scooches his chair over to us with a heavy scrape on the floor, and begins rubbing baby boy's back, leaning his temple against our angel's shoulder.

"Do you really love me, Daddy?" baby boy asks in a small, strained voice.

My heart twists. "I love you so much," I say without hesitation before kissing the top of his head. I reach for my big man's hand and squeeze it, sharing a look with him. "Both of you. I meant what I said back there. You're mine. I couldn't imagine it any other way."

"Hell to the yeah," big man says with his signature enthusiasm. Baby boy peeks out at him, and my heart melts as they share a sweet kiss. "I don't have no doubt all the gods got together and sent you to us, cherub."

Baby boy bites his lip, and his eyes shine with sadness. "Not my mother's god," he says quietly.

Big man frowns. "I don't know about your mom's god, baby boy," he says seriously. "But my momma and our whole family go to church every single Sunday. Some folks there might not understand the likes of me or us, but I know with my whole heart Momma, Pops, and all my siblings are gonna love the shit out of you. Our god loves you."

Pride wells up in me, and I squeeze his hand again. "That he does," I agree. I shift in my seat. "I know I don't talk much about my religion. My family are more culturally Jewish than practicing. But one thing I know for sure is that God—my god—made us all in his imagine. You are exactly who you are supposed to be because you have God within you. My bubbe would say you have a divine spark. So of course he loves you. You're perfect."

For a moment, baby boy just stays quiet. Then he takes in a shaky breath. "Thank you. I love you both so much. I don't care that I've never had a boyfriend or anything. It's like I only had half a life before. Half a heart. Now I'm so full and alive. But...what about the holidays? Or graduation?"

"What about them?" I ask, gently brushing some of his golden curls back from his forehead.

He blinks up at me. "What happens after?"

"I guess it depends on where Daddy gets signed," big man says thoughtfully. I'm overwhelmed with fondness for him. There's no 'if' when it comes to me getting signed as far as he's concerned.

Baby boy still looks anxious, though. "You mean…you'd still want to keep seeing me?"

Coldness washes through me along with a spike of anger that the universe could possibly even consider taking my boy away from me.

"Of course we do," I say, pleased that big man looks just as horrified as I feel.

"I assumed we'd try and find a place to live together," he says as if that was obvious. "I know it depends on a bunch of stuff and it might take a while. Baby boy gets accommodation with his scholarship, after all. So—"

He's interrupted as our angel bursts into messy tears, clinging to me like I'm a life raft out in choppy waters.

"Little dude!" big man cries out in confusion.

"I thought…you were both…going to leave me," he manages to rasp between sobs.

"What?" I snap, probably harsher than I should. "Why would you have ever thought that, angel? I told you. You're mine now. I'm not going to just toss you away because circumstances change a little."

"We would never do that, cherub," big man adds, sounding hurt. He rubs baby boy's back as our little one continues to sniffle. "I don't know what I'd do without you. You're my sunshine. Everything's better with you and Daddy around."

Baby boy wipes his eyes and blinks at us with spiky lashes. "Are you serious?" he asks weakly.

I frown. "Would Daddy lie to you?" I ask sternly.

Thankfully, that seems to give him the permission he needs to stop questioning our intentions. "No, Daddy," he says softly, burrowing down farther against my chest.

"Exactly," I say, some of my own tension easing. I know I can't make him stay if that's not what he wants, but I'm damn well not leaving him, not while I still have breath in my body. "It's Daddy Zeus, Papa Dionysus, and our angel boy sent from the heavens. We're a team."

He bites his lip, then nods. "Okay," he says.

I'm tired, so I figure my boys must be exhausted. The adrenaline that was running through my veins after the game seems to have finally left my system, and I'm ready to cuddle up with my favorite people and go the fuck to sleep.

We can worry about the future tomorrow. The only thing that really matters is that we'll be facing it together. I feel sick that I let our baby down and he thought this was only some kind of arrangement that lasted until graduation. Moving forward, I'll know to do better. Be more vigilant.

He's right, after all. I might not have had a boyfriend before, but I know that I'm in love with these two very different guys. I care about graduation and going pro still, sure. But if it comes to a choice between all that and them, I'd live out of a cardboard box to make sure we stay together.

Like baby boy said to that woman who abandoned him: I choose love. I choose happiness. What's life without those things?

"Come on," I urge him, giving him a nudge. "Let's take this upstairs. It's been a long enough day. We can tackle anything else tomorrow. Now we need to sleep."

"And cuddles?" big man asks hopefully.

I laugh, and even baby boy gives a weak chuckle. Good, hopefully he's slowly pulling himself out of his funk.

"All the cuddles," I promise.

As we stand, I shrug off my Panthers letter jacket and drape it over baby boy's shoulders. He looks down at it, then back up at me with wide eyes.

"That's yours now," I tell him. "You're one of the team. Our good luck charm."

"I couldn't," he protests. "It means so much to you. Besides, it's way too big on me."

"That's what makes it so hot," big man says, nodding his head and raising his eyebrows.

I snort. Always with his mind on one thing, that boy. "It did mean a lot to me," I agree. "Being captain of this team has been an honor. But I'm about to start a new chapter of my life, and you mean more to me. I want you to have it."

He wraps himself up in it, inhaling my scent from the collar. "I love it, Daddy. Thank you."

Big man wraps his arms around him and makes him squeak as he picks him up. "I'll figure something to give you as well, darlin'," he promises as baby boy wraps his legs around big man's solid torso. "But I think whatever it is will probably need washing first."

I laugh properly at that. "That sounds like a very sensible idea."

He beams at me as we make our way to the stairs, him still carrying baby boy. "See? Not such a clown anymore. I'm full of knowledge and sensible ideas."

I lean over to kiss him before we start our ascent. "I wouldn't go that far," I tell him warmly. "I still like you goofy. You just know who you are now. No more pretending."

"You're my Papa," baby boy pipes up. "And my Daddy. Mine."

"Yours," I agree wholeheartedly.

"Yours," big man repeats.

I don't know exactly what the future holds, but one thing's for sure, and that's the fact that I'll have these two amazing guys by my side. As we fall asleep that night, all cuddling together in a pile of limbs and warm, minty breath, I know I don't have to worry.

The details are in the hands of the gods. All that matters is that we love each other.

Now and forever.

# CHAPTER 21

## *Gabe*

### SIX MONTHS LATER

"Martin Patrick Quinn," the dean's voice calls out over the sound system.

It would be impossible to compete with the horde of Texans who jump to their feet in the graduation day crowd, screaming and hollering as Papa jogs up to the stage. But I certainly try. I cheer and clap, a lump in my throat as tears of joy threaten to tumble down my cheeks. I see Daddy also standing up amid their graduating class, clapping hard as Papa shakes the dean's hand and takes his rolled-up diploma.

Daddy's surname starts with an 'E,' so he's already got his.

Because of course they've both graduated. My Daddies. My Gods. I'm so proud of them both I could burst. I knew they could do it.

The rest of the ceremony seems to drag on forever, even though we're near the end of the alphabet. I know it's because I'm impatient to see my Daddies, but I'm also quite anxious about meeting their families again.

Just like we told my mother, we spent the holidays together. But because everything was so raw, we just told everyone that we were friends. I know I was quiet and with-drawn despite both families' kindness and generosity. I was still in such a state of shock that my parents really had disowned me.

We only stayed for the most important days in Chicago and Texas, then made our way back to Paddle Creek to cele-brate New Year's with the rest of Daddy's frat house, many of whom hadn't gone home for the holidays either.

In some ways, it can seriously suck being LGBT. But in others, it's awesome. Alpha Zeta Kappa is a family, and no one gets left behind.

None of us three want to live in the closet, though, so Daddy and Papa have both since come clean and explained exactly what we are to one another. Both families have been warned that they're being introduced to two boyfriends today.

Apparently, Daddy's parents were a little surprised but came around to the idea pretty quickly. Papa's dad didn't seem to understand, but told him 'S'long as you're happy, son, that's a-okay with me.' But his mom screamed at him down the phone, saying things like 'I always knew you had too much love in you to give, sweetie!' and 'You go! That's my boy!'

Papa's face when he told us was so adorable, filled with pride and love and relief. I guess today's when we'll find out if they're all really okay with everything.

As the long ceremony mercifully ends, the crowd rises to their feet and begins to shuffle out of the large auditorium. I was sitting by myself near the back and quickly lose sight of Daddy and Papa in the sea of people. We'd agreed to meet up outside by the big oak tree, so that's where I head to. My Daddies are probably going to take a minute collecting their families, so I can just chill and try and ignore my nerves.

I lean against the big tree and I rub my fingers against the tiny burlap bag in my pocket. I've still never opened it. However, I carry it pretty much wherever I go these days. I might not believe in whatever it is that Ms. Maude does, but her gift certainly reminds me of the kindness the people in this town can bestow.

As if summoned to remind me that Paddle Creek isn't perfect, though, I look up to realize that Logan McKenna is approaching me, and I stiffen.

He stops a few feet away from me, his lips pursed and his eyes narrowed. Then he shrugs. "You won," he says. "I can admit it."

It's my turn to narrow my eyes. I've seen him around this past semester, but I haven't spoken to him since the night my mother disowned me. It's never been confirmed, but we're all pretty convinced it was him who got my RA to call Mama and feed her some ridiculous story about me getting into trouble so she could come and catch me in all my 'sin.'

In a way, I can see that it's all worked out for the best. I immediately felt the improvement in my life without the daily draining phone calls from her and the heavy weight of a future I desperately didn't want no longer dragging me down. I can't say exactly what's going to happen moving forward, but if she can't accept me for who I am and who I love, then I think I'll be okay with being disowned. The ball's in her court if she wants to change her mind.

My father never even reached out to me. I always suspected if I ever came out then he'd disown me without a second thought, but that doesn't mean it didn't hurt like hell when it actually happened. For eighteen years, I was their world.

Then I was nothing.

I've sort of managed to convince myself that if that's how

they really feel, it's probably better that I know now. My life is already better without them.

But none of what happened was on my terms. I was essentially forced out of the closet by Logan's actions. That's something I can never take back.

On the other hand, he's totally right. I did win. If it weren't for him, I never would have met my Daddies and become the happiest angel on the whole of planet Earth.

"I did," I say curtly, not making any move to shake his hand or even leave. *He* can leave. This is where I agreed to meet my Daddies and their families, so this is where I'm going to stay. I'm done bending myself into painful shapes for people who don't deserve it.

He reaches inside his graduation gown and retrieves a thick white envelope. He offers it to me. "Well, a bet's a bet."

For a second, I just blink at him. Then I realize of course he means the money. I'd completely forgotten there was three *thousand* dollars riding on my Daddies graduating.

The moment stretches out as I think of what that cash might have meant to us even just a few months ago. But then I swallow and shake my head. "No, thank you," I say, doing my best not to let my voice shake.

He raises his eyebrows. "Huh?"

I shake my head again. "I like that you honored the terms of the bet, but no, thank you. We don't want or need your money."

He scoffs and looks at me like I'm insane. "The hell? Yes, you do. You're all poor as fuck. You can't eat pride, Visoth. Just take the damn cash."

I push myself off the tree and stand up tall. I refuse to lose my temper. Daddy wouldn't like that. But I do square my shoulders and glare up at the spoiled rich kid who thinks he can buy his way out of any situation.

"I guess you didn't hear," I say, my voice cold and smooth despite the triumph that wants to bubble up. "Daddy's already been signed by the Spartans. We'll be perfectly fine, thank you very much."

From the look on Logan's face, it's likely he had indeed not heard that news. He swallows, his jaw pinched, slowly retracting his hand and putting the cash away again.

"I see," he says curtly.

"If I might offer some advice?" I say calmly. "Stop living your life trying to impress other people. Choose happiness. Be real. Be kind. That way, you might discover you're not as mean and bitter as you thought."

He sneers and rolls his eyes. "As if I'd take advice from a little pervert like you. Have a nice life in this crappy town, Visoth."

"I intend to," I say softly as I watch him retreat.

I would have made a quip about how this town might be crappy, but at least *my* family doesn't own it. Surely, it's the McKennas fault that nothing here works and everything is at least two decades old. But in the past couple of weeks, they've mysteriously withdrawn their bid to rename the Panthers' football stadium as well as stepping away from several other projects. The official word is that they want to 'invest in a more profitable region.'

I have a feeling it's more that when the star quarterback gets signed to a NFL team, the college board and town council are suddenly a lot more interested in honoring *his* wishes.

Daddy might not be rich and famous just yet, but he's certainly on his way. Unlike the McKennas, though, I know he'll never abuse his power, and I doubt he'll forget Paddle Creek when he gets to the top, either.

"Gabe!" Daddy's voice calls out, immediately making me

look away from the vanishing form of Logan McKenna and forgetting him, probably forever.

He doesn't matter. He's the past.

My Daddies are the future.

My heart skips a beat as I see them both marching toward me, their families following behind them. They look so handsome in their black graduation caps and gowns. My pulse starts racing with nerves at the prospect of meeting their families again now the truth is out, but I don't really get a chance to fret before Daddy and Papa both envelop me in their arms.

"Hey, angel," Daddy says against my ear.

"Congratulations!" I squeak at both of them. "You looked so fantastic up on that stage. I was so proud!"

They both kiss the top of my head and then let me go. I blush as I see all the people who have crowded around us. Daddy just has his parents and one of his grandmas. But Papa has almost ten family members, and they all seem to be vibrating with excitement.

"Marty says it's all thanks to you that he was up on that there stage," says Papa's Momma. She yanks me from my Daddies into a crushing hug. "You boys are plain awful, not tellin' us you were all really datin'. And you being just as cute as a button. Gosh, how thrillin'!"

I laugh as she lets me go, blushing even harder. "Oh, no, ma'am. Marty mostly got himself on that stage. I just gave him a little extra help at the end."

"Nonsense," Daddy says with a frown. "We were both in serious trouble. Your tutoring was lifesaving."

He wraps his arm around my back, and so does Papa. I feel lightheaded and slightly panicky as I glance at all the people observing us. But no one acts shocked or scandalized. In fact, Daddy's parents hug side by side, watching on fondly. "You three look so happy," his dad says.

"Don't they just?" Papa's momma says.

"Right!" his pops declares with a clap of his hands. "I'm starving. Are we celebrating these crazy kids or what?"

Daddy grins at me and Papa. "Oh, we're definitely going to be celebrating," he says.

I gulp, hardly able to wait for what he's got in store.

# CHAPTER 22

## *Gabe*

DINNER WAS WONDERFUL. I REALLY DIDN'T NEED TO WORRY at all.

Papa's family is staying at the motel in town, but Daddy's parents are at the fancy hotel in between Paddle Creek and Albertson. We'd heard their restaurant did a mean steak, so we all went out there for a fantastic evening of celebration. Daddy's parents were a little reserved but very kind. Papa's momma was calling me 'son' before our main courses even came out.

It's not like I can ever expect to replace my own family. If this is the way things stay, I'll just have to come to terms with that. But the affection I got from these near strangers tonight would have been quite unbelievable if I didn't already know how much Daddy and Papa love me.

In many ways, I'm the luckiest boy alive.

After we parted ways, Daddy's mom drove us to the nearest trolley stop, and we headed back into town to head to Creams along with every other graduating queer in town. A drag queen called Kimmi Sugar lit the small stage on fire with her comedy and lip-syncing, and I danced the night away with my Daddies, feeling like I was floating on cloud nine. We'd drunk some wine with dinner, but the club was such a workout, all any of us wanted was water.

Which turned out to be a very good thing.

We tumble through the door of Daddy's frat house at just past one in the morning. There's a party going on in the living room, but Daddy shoos me and Papa up the stairs while he mysteriously disappears into the kitchen.

"What do you think he's getting?" I ask Papa, looking over my shoulder as we climb up to the top floor.

Papa blinks and tries far too hard to look innocent. "No idea, angel."

I snort and shake my head. I guess I'll find out soon enough either way.

Daddy is moving out tomorrow, so this will be the last night we ever spend in his room. I'm sad to be saying goodbye to the place where we shared so many firsts. Where we fell in love. But I'm also *so* excited about what the future is going to bring.

Papa sits on the end of the bed and hugs me against him between his legs. I cradle his head against my chest, and he sighs. "I told you they'd love you, didn't I?" he says, sounding like he's more musing out loud rather than asking an actual question. "And Daddy. Damn, I was nervous. I know y'all met at Christmas, but this was different. I knew they accepted me bein' gay and all, but two boyfriends was a bit of a thing to surprise 'em with. It all went okay, though, didn't it, angel?"

I smile and kiss his forehead. "It was more than okay. It was amazing. I didn't know you were nervous."

"I just wanted them to like y'all so badly," he says, looking up at me with his big brown eyes. He's such a human puppy. It makes my heart melt. "And you to like them. Now it feels like my world is complete."

It's on the tip of my tongue to apologize again for my

mother's behavior. I would have given anything for her to love and approve of my relationship with my two men. But it's not meant to be, so that's that. I make a vow in that moment to let go of the past once and for all.

"You and Daddy are my whole world," I promise him. "And my heaven above. I'm really, really glad your families like me—and I like them. It feels like fate brought us all together."

He grins and kisses my lips. "It really does."

"There are my boys," Daddy says fondly as he comes through the door.

I look over from the foot of the bed, watching him shut and lock the door behind him. I frown, trying to work out what he's carrying. It looks like one of the many boxes from the grocery store in town that the guys who are moving out are in the midst of packing with. But it has a large, folded-up towel draped over the top of it. That's not what I expected him to come from the kitchen with.

He comes and sits beside Papa, a huge grin on his face that makes me excited but also kind of nervous. He places the box a little behind him so it doesn't slide off the bed.

"We've got a present for you, baby boy," he announces.

My eyebrows jump up. "Wait, no! I should have gotten *you* guys presents," I cry in mild horror.

Papa scoffs. "No way, darlin'. *You're* our present."

"Every day," Daddy agrees. "You can think of this as your graduation ceremony, though, if you prefer. We had ours today, and so should you."

"We're going to take you to the Ice Cream Parlor," Papa adds, waggling his eyebrows.

I frown in confusion. "But…that's where we just came from."

They both laugh, but not unkindly. Daddy takes the towel off the box and leans it forward to let me peek inside. My eyes go wide. I guess Papa wasn't kidding. There's a tub of cherry-flavored ice cream in there, along with a can of whipped cream, chocolate sauce, sprinkles, and a couple of spoons.

Okay. I've officially turned into the sexual deviant that everybody keeps telling me I am. I thought it was going to be fluffy handcuffs or something.

I repress a shiver. *Should* I ask Daddy for handcuffs? That sounds…hot. Like really hot. I wouldn't be able to get away. I'd be at his mercy as he and Papa fucked me senseless. Oh…Gods…

I mentally shake myself and smile. This is their special day, and I'm definitely not going to be an ungrateful brat. "Yum!" I say enthusiastically.

Daddy's smile is smoldering, and my tummy flips over. "Oh, you might get a taste, baby boy," he says teasingly. "But this is for me and Papa."

He raises his eyebrows expectantly, and heat rises in my cheeks. I think I'm missing something here. That seems a bit mean, even for Daddy if they're going to make me watch them eat ice cream and not give me some. I look back inside the box to see how many bowls there are…but there aren't any.

Oh.

*OH!*

I stop blushing in embarrassment, my skin flaming with desire instead as it dawns on me what they mean.

They want to eat all that *off me.*

My Daddies watch me hungrily as I finally connect the dots. I bite my thumbnail and try not to squirm.

"You want to make me into a human sundae?" I say.

Daddy drops his head back and laughs. Papa just nods eagerly.

"That's it, baby boy," Daddy says warmly. "We popped

your cherry. Now you get to *be* the cherry."

I love it when he mixes up metaphors because what he's saying is always either hot or sweet, and that's just so him. Technically in this scenario, I'd be the bowl or the plate, but I like the idea of being their cherry better.

"I'll be so tasty for you, Daddy. I promise," I tell him breathlessly.

He growls and slips his hand around my neck to pull me down for a kiss. "I know you will, angel. But this is just the foreplay. Tonight, for your actual graduation, Papa and I are going to fuck your sweet hole at the same time. Do you think you can manage that?"

I'm not sure what he's asking me. They always fuck me together…

Oh. Oh, hang on. He doesn't mean everybody having sex at the same time, does he? He means…

My heart skips a beat, and for a second, I panic.

Double penetration.

Papa is already so big. How could Daddy possibly get in there at the same time?

I force myself to slow down and think. I've been watching videos—a *lot* of videos—and I know how far it's possible to stretch a hole with time and effort. I'm already so much better at taking Papa compared to when we first started. I know my Daddies would never hurt me in a bad way, only in a fun way. If they think I can do this, I want to try.

I let out the breath I was holding and nod. "I can do it, Daddy," I say, already feeling my blood pumping. "I'll be the sweetest treat."

Papa groans and also pulls me down for a messy kiss. "Yes, you will, cherub."

They both stand, and Daddy spreads the towel on top of his bed covers, presumably to catch the mess. Then he and Papa both undress me slowly, taking their time to kiss and touch every single part of my body. I giggle and moan as they do, feeling perfectly adored. Once I'm totally naked, they help me to lie down on the towel on my back.

They're both still dressed, and it makes me feel shy and vulnerable but in the best kind of way. You'd think they'd have all the power, but I know that I do.

Just like Persephone.

I bite my lip and shiver as Daddy pops the lid off the melting ice cream and takes a spoonful to drizzle it onto my tummy. He flicks his eyebrows at Papa, who bends down and licks it off like it's cum. I gasp and jerk, so Daddy takes my hands and puts them above the bed. There's nothing to hold on to, but I can pretend there is.

"You stay still for your Daddies, now," he says firmly.

I nod. "Next time," I say, feeling brave, "you can tie me up, Daddy. Then you could do whatever you want with me."

Both he and Papa freeze with wide eyes.

"Oh, *baby* boy," Daddy groans, leaning down for a filthy kiss. "I think I know how we're going to christen the new bed."

I wriggle in delight until I remember that I'm supposed to be staying still.

It's not easy, though.

Daddy drops two freezing cold dollops of the cherry ice cream onto my sensitive nipples which he and Papa suck clean, making the buds hard and tender. Papa amuses himself greatly by covering my hard cock in whipped cream and sprinkles before devouring it all. Daddy keeps playing with the cold ice cream, making me shiver and whimper as he drizzles it along my arms, in the dip of my throat, and in my belly button, lapping it from my skin as it melts. Papa pushes my knees up and covers my hole in chocolate sauce, getting it all over his face as he stretches me out with his tongue.

My cock is already throbbing, leaking precum into the

remnants of the cream. Daddy has a packet of wet wipes so that he and Papa can clean their faces and hands, maintaining their dignity. But I'm a sticky, writhing mess by the time Papa starts fingering me, getting me ready for my biggest challenge yet.

"Good boy," Daddy murmurs as he smears chocolate sauce over his length, then straddles my shoulders to feed it to me. "Daddy told you that you'd get a little treat, too," he says as he rubs the tip against my lips.

"It's not little, Daddy," I say, making him laugh before he pushes it inside my mouth. I love how genuine and filthy his moan is as I suck and lick it. It's both sweet and salty, like chocolate-covered pretzels.

He fucks my mouth until Papa's gotten three fingers inside my hole. "I think our angel's ready, Daddy," he says. I watch, my mouth full of cock, as Daddy leans back to kiss him over his shoulder.

"Sure thing, big man," he rasps, his voice sending shivers down my spine.

I *love* hearing how they're going to fuck me, like it's inevitable, and I don't have a choice. Of course I do. I can always use my safe words. But feeling like I'm their plaything —like I really was made by the gods to be filled by their cocks—sends me floating into this kind of trance that I yearn for.

We move around into a new position. Daddy cleans around my mouth as Papa lies down, his monster cock bobbing and leaking, like it's excited to finally be played with. I straddle him and bite my lip as I slide myself down onto it. Yet again, I wonder if I can really do this. Yes, I can stretch myself around his epic girth now...but can Daddy really fit in there as well?

I'm sure he senses my nerves as he kneels beside me and runs his fingers through my hair, scratching the back of my neck. "It's okay, bubbelah," he whispers to me, kissing along my jaw and nipping my earlobe. "Take it nice and slow. You can do this. You're being so brave and beautiful for your Daddies."

I whimper, and he presses his mouth to mine. Papa leans up and joins us. I love our messy three-way kisses, and it helps me to relax. I need to stop worrying about how I'm going to do this and just let it happen.

When I'm nice and stretched around Papa's length, he thrusts leisurely, hitting my prostate and making me squeal and jerk as pleasure rips through my body. Then Daddy's behind me, lube-drenched fingers stroking the top of my hole as Papa slides against it.

"Are you ready, angel?" Daddy asks.

I bite my lip and breathe heavily through my nose. "Um-hm," I squeak, nodding frantically.

I gasp and try not to freeze up as he eases a single finger through my tight ring of muscle. But as I breathe and do my best to let go of my tension, I realize the burn really isn't that bad. I guess I've already been stretched so much already. I was imagining it was going to be like when I first accepted Papa inside me and the invasion felt so alien to my body.

I take a couple more breaths and nod, looking between Papa beneath me and Daddy behind me. "I'm okay," I say. Both my voice and my arms are trembling where they're holding me up, but I mean it. "I can take more."

"Good boy," Daddy says earnestly, kissing the back of my neck. "Daddy's so proud of you. You're amazing."

I hiss as he fits a second digit inside, but the burn is just as manageable as before.

I'm ready. I'm really going to be fucked by two big God cocks like the divine slut I am.

"Daddy, I need you," I say, panting desperately. "Please. *Please.*"

"Shh, it's okay, baby boy," he says with deep affection. He strokes my side with his dry hand, then withdraws the other one. I feel the mattress shifting behind me and hear him squeezing more lube out. Then his back is pressed against mine, and I can feel the blunt head of his dick probing against the top of my hole. "I'm going to fuck you now, sweetheart. I'm going to use your hole and Papa's beast of a cock to make us both come inside you. And you're going to love it, aren't you?"

"I am. I am!" I cry, shaking with damp eyes. "I'm yours, Daddy. Use me. Fuck me!"

"What are you?" he asks, his voice dangerously low as he starts to push inside.

"A s-slut," I manage to utter. "Your angel slut."

"That's right, gorgeous. And who do you belong to?"

"Daddy and Papa. My Gods!"

"Who are you going to come for?"

"Daddy and Papa."

"Who do you love?"

*"Daddy and Papa!"* I gasp and squirm as he bottoms out. I'm so full I feel like I'm going to be turned inside out. It's impossible. But it's happening.

"Good boy," Papa says, his face beaming as he leans up to capture my mouth for a kiss. "You feel so fucking amazing. I knew you could do it. How amazing is Daddy's cock?"

"So good. So, *so* good. Fuck me, both of you, *please.*"

They start to move, and it's almost too much. The rhythm starts off messy. Sometimes they thrust at the same time, then they'll switch to nailing me one after the other. The ridges of their cocks pull at my hole. My prostate feels like it's getting jackhammered. I wail and bounce and cling on to Papa's broad shoulders. Daddy grips my hips where I seem to be permanently bruised these days.

I love it.

It seems he has marking me on his mind. He sucks and bites at the side of my neck, no doubt trying to leave a hickey. He's never done that before, but I guess the semester's over, and none of us has anything to lose. Even better, he reaches down and scratches along Papa's side, making him hiss and his eyes roll into the back of his head like when Daddy spanks him. He loves the sharp sting, I'm sure, and it sends a spike of lust through me to see it.

*"Mine,"* Daddy snarls, fucking me harder. *"Mine, mine, MINE."*

He seizes my shoulders as his orgasm rips through him, and I feel him throbbing inside me. He's still thrusting. They both are. Papa pumps hard a few more times, but then he's also screwing up his face, spilling his seed, filling me up to the brim.

I gasp and shiver as they stay there for a few moments, catching their breaths and softening inside me. I'm still hard and leaking, but I'm not even sure I have the energy to come now. I feel utterly wrung out and like I'm floating on another plane of existence.

But Daddy slowly pulls out of me, then helps ease me off Papa's length. He lays me down in between them, and they take turns kissing my lips and neck. I can feel myself leaking from behind onto the towel. It's perfectly decadent.

"Such a good angel for your Gods," Daddy murmurs, wrapping his hand around my cock. "It's okay, cherub. You can let go now. Come for us."

It only takes a few strokes for me to erupt, spraying myself with hot, sticky cum. I sob as Daddy milks the last drops from me, all the while telling me how good and beautiful and perfect I am.

This right here is heaven, between my amazing Daddy Gods.

And I'm never going to let them go.

# Epilogue

## ONE YEAR LATER – GABE

"Whoa."

I shield my eyes from the sun as I gaze out over the impressive terrain. Papa wraps his arms around my waist and cuddles me from behind, inhaling and sighing happily.

"Truly a gift from the gods," he agrees.

I still can't actually believe we're in Greece. I've read so much about the ancient culture, philosophy, history, and of course the gods. I feel like I've lived and breathed Mount Olympus for years.

Now I'm standing on it.

We decided to go on our first vacation outside of America after Daddy completed his rookie season with the Spartans. In fact, Daddy and Papa surprised me with the news on Valentine's Day, following it up with some particularly filthy sex that left me sore for days in so many places in the best possible way.

It felt so right that we should come to Greece. The fact that we could afford to do so on Daddy's new salary was almost too good to be true. I think of how important that three-thousand-dollar bet had seemed at the time. We would have been totally within our rights to have still taken the money from Logan. But my Daddies agreed that I did the right thing. It was so much better to start the next chapter of our lives without anything to do with him.

Because the training facility for the Spartans is only a forty-five-minute drive away, Daddy and Papa agreed to rent a place in Paddle Creek while I finish out my degree. After that, we'll have a little more freedom to move around, but I have to say I've fallen more and more in love with our slightly ramshackle town. I can see it being home for a long time to come.

Especially as Papa has also gotten a job in town that he loves. He's coaching football to tiny kindergarteners. He's *so* good with them it melts my heart. Mostly he just plays catch with them and gets them to run into squishy pads with adorable little helmets on, but to see the way those tiny tots' confidence has risen is really something.

There's one little girl who didn't even want to pick up the ball to begin with. She was only there because her twin brother was desperate to play. But it turns out she's got an arm like a catapult. Now the twosome terrorizes their way across the field and I'm pretty sure she's going to try and play on her school team with the boys when she's older, and honestly, I fear for them a little bit.

As for me, school is going fantastically. I'm no longer worried about having to take any business or finance classes and have just lost myself in classics. Professor Knight is already talking to me about doing a masters and after that maybe even a career in academia.

It seems too good to be true that I could mess around with my books for a living, but he's got so many museum connections from his time in the UK and says he also works with people in film and television as a consultant. These are all things I could do as well. I love that he's taken me under his wing.

Of course nothing in life is perfect. My mother stayed true to her word and I haven't heard from her since, other than receiving a couple of boxes of stuff sent from my home in Missouri to the university mailroom, which was both embarrassing and terribly sad. Sometimes I still cry about it, but I don't think I'm actually missing her or my father. I'm mourning the parents and the relationship I always hoped I'd get one day if I just tried hard enough. But I was never going to get it. They were never going to love me the way I deserved or accept me for who I am, so I'm slowly leaving them behind and flourishing in my new, amazing life.

I was supposed to stay in the college dorms for my second year. However, Daddy also surprised me there to let me know I'd been accepted into Alpha Zeta Kappa. I tried to protest that I wasn't on the team, but the guys had all insisted that I'd earned my place with them after the way I'd helped Daddy and Papa to graduate. Now I'm friends with the people I used to follow on Instagram. They're not statistics anymore. They're my brothers.

As a thank you, I finally got to spruce up that crappy front porch. Not only has it got a new lick of paint, but potted plants and even a rocking chair.

I belong. I have family. And *this* holiday season, we were able to spend it with both Daddy's and Papa's families while being out and proud. No more hiding or second-guessing. Just a couple of houses full of love. And thanks to Daddy's amazing salary, we treated ourselves and spent New Year's in New York and had a truly spectacular time out on the town.

We even went to Chicago for Passover in the spring, and we're probably going to head to Texas for Thanksgiving in the fall. I think Papa's momma and Daddy's mom are secretly trying to see who can fatten me up the most with all their amazing food, and I can't say I'm mad about it.

Losing my relationship with my parents still hurts, but it's tolerable when I'm surrounded by so many people who cherish me and value me for exactly who I am.

I split my time between the frat house and the apartment, but lately, I've been at the apartment every second I can. This has everything to do with the kitten we adopted from Nim, the scary biker who runs Toe Beans. She's a feisty little ginger that we named Artemis, the Greek goddess of hunting. I've never had a pet before, but this little lady has stolen my heart in a way I never could have imagined. I almost didn't want to go on vacation and leave her behind for two weeks, but Dukey promised to look after her really well for us.

I'm so glad we did come, and Artemis will be waiting when we get home. Greece has been everything I ever dreamed of and more. We've been staying in Athens, where we've seen and done so many things. In order to visit Mount Olympus, we rented a car and drove a few hours north to a little town called Litochoro, where the mountain trail starts.

We've been walking all day, and we'll have to stay at one of the refuges along the way overnight, but so far, it's been completely worth it. The views of the wide lakes, deep valleys, and colorful meadows have been astonishing. We even passed by the ruins of the Dionysus Monastery, where we stopped to take loads of photos with Papa that won't mean much to anyone aside from us, but that's okay. It's our special inside joke.

As Papa and I gaze out over the incredible vista, Daddy comes and joins us, hugging me as well as we take in the view. But I can feel he's tense, and after a while, I turn and look at both my Gods with a frown.

"Is everything okay, Daddy?" I ask.

We're far enough away from the rest of the hiking group that I wouldn't be overheard, but honestly, over the past year and a half, I've cared less and less about who hears me call Daddy and Papa by their names anyway.

He smiles. "I can't hide anything from you, can I, baby boy? Yes, everything's fine. Magnificent, in fact. I just have a present for you and big man. It's something for all three of us, actually."

"Presents?" Papa repeats excitably, making me giggle.

"Why would presents make you nervous, Daddy?" I ask. "I'm sure we'll love them."

He bites his lip, and rather than answer right away, he reaches into his pocket and gets out a small, velvet-covered box.

My heart skips a beat.

My shock probably shows on my face because he laughs again and shakes his head ruefully. "That's why I was nervous. Don't worry, I don't have a question to ask anyone. Not today, anyway. That's sort of the point. But I wanted to make a promise for the time being. I wanted to show my men how much I love them."

"We know you love us, Daddy," I say reproachfully.

Papa elbows me in the ribs. "Shh, baby boy. This love comes with a *present*."

Daddy and I both chuckle fondly. Then Daddy opens up the rectangular box.

I gasp again, but this time softly in awe rather than in shock. It's a ring box, just like I thought. But inside are nestled three rings in a line together. I lean closer to take a better look.

They're all gold, and the bands are made of tiny leaves laid over one another, like the laurel wreaths the ancient Greeks gave out in their Olympic Games. Where the tips of the wreaths meet in the middle, each ring has a different symbol. A lightning bolt for Zeus, two touching wine glasses for Dionysus, and the last one has an oblong circle. It takes me a second to realize that of course it's an angel's halo.

They couldn't be more perfect, and I feel my eyes well up with tears. "I love them, Daddy," I manage to whisper. I look over at Papa and let out a wet chuckle when I see he's not goofing around anymore in that moment. He's also got glassy eyes and has covered his mouth with his hand.

Daddy lets out a relieved breath, puffing out his cheeks. "Thank fuck for that," he mutters as he pulls out my ring first. "That was the scariest thing I've ever done."

I laugh again and rub my eyes with my free hand, holding out my right one so Daddy can slip the ring onto the correct finger. When we're all wearing them, we touch our fingertips together, admiring how they glint in the Greek sunshine.

"Mine," Daddy says simply.

"Mine," Papa agrees.

"Mine," I say with a nod. "Yours."

"Yours," my Gods repeat back to me.

I say a silent prayer to Aphrodite, thankful to her every day for the path in life that brought our souls together. I know Daddy doesn't want to do anything drastic while we're all still so young, but I know what he's trying to say.

Fate brought us together, and that's the way I know we're going to stay. Forever in this life and into the world beyond.

Because I can't imagine a heaven that doesn't have my Daddies in it.

---

Thank you so much for reading Seth, Marty, and Gabe's story!

**Two men. Two secrets. Can true love set them free?**

Make sure you don't miss the next

Paddle Creek College book featuring Professor Knight and his sassy TA Jackson. *Yes, Sir* is coming January 2023.

**Pre-order your copy now!**

If you want more small towns or Daddies, make sure you keep reading for other books by HJ Welch/Helen Juliet.

———

If you'd like to be the first to know what's happening next in Paddle Creek, make sure to join my Facebook group, **Helen's Jewels**. We also have a lot of fun with games and giveaways, as well as ARC opportunities.

———

Thank you to my team!

Cover Design: Cate Ashwood

Editing: Meg Cooper (you really went above and beyond with this one with all the football and college stuff—thank you!)

Proof Reading: Tanja Ongkiehong

Witchy advice: Elizabeth Silver

Jewish consultant: Rena Yehuda Newman

General awesomeness: Ed Davies, AK Faulkner, my hubby, and our cats.

## THREE BY HELEN JULIET

**All good things come in threes…**

When three shy best friends sign up to a dating app to finally lose their virginity by the end of the year, they don't expect to all fall for the same gorgeous, slightly scary-looking Daddy. The only solution? Let him choose who he wants to bed. Except he doesn't…

Jacob didn't become a billionaire before hitting thirty-five by making compromises. What he wants, he *gets.* So why should he choose between these adorable boys when he can devour all three? Instead, he tells them to decide on an order, and then he'll spoil each of them one after the other in a way they'll never forget.

Will one night each be enough? And can that really be all they need to fall in love? One thing's for sure, when danger comes calling, this Daddy will discover just how far he'll go to protect his three little piggies.

*Three* is a super steamy, standalone MMMM gay romance novel featuring a Daddy wolf ready to huff and puff his way into three hearts, best friends who discover something more between them, a box full of abandoned kittens, and a guaranteed HEA with absolutely no cliffhanger.

**Click here to get the Three eBook**

**DADDY**

Goldie is shy, innocent, brand-new…and totally irresistible. I'm going to make him ours. The three of us have enough love for a fourth. It's supposed to be only for a weekend, but our golden angel's secrets betray a broken soul that needs mending…and I'm the man to do it. Goldie's sleazy ex is too cold for him, and this weekend might be too hot. But the four of us together? That feels just right. And when I find out why Goldie's really there, we'll stop at nothing to save our golden boy.

*Golden* is a super steamy, standalone MMMM gay romance novella featuring a picturesque cottage in the English countryside, lashings of praise for a shy boy, one very fat cat who knows best, enough porridge for four hungry tummies, and a guaranteed HEA with absolutely no cliffhanger.

**Click here to get the Golden eBook**

I've never been anyone's Daddy before, but Red needs me in a way that melts my grizzly heart. I'll do anything for him. But if my recent, brutal divorce has taught me anything, it's that I'm not much of a catch. Does a beautiful young thing like Red really want me? His brother might be my best friend, but his father hates us both and will do all he can to keep us apart. When trouble comes knocking on my door, though, I know I'll do anything to save this boy I've fallen for.

*Wild Ride* is a super steamy, standalone MM gay romance novella featuring a boy who discovers a love of lingerie, a sassy grandma, a loyal pooch the size of a wolf, something scary lurking in the woods, and a guaranteed HEA with absolutely no cliffhanger.

**Click here to get the Wild Ride eBook**

**NINE LIVES BY HELEN JULIET**

## CHARLIE

I'm in trouble with a capital T. Thanks to my no-good stepfather, I suddenly find myself penniless, homeless, and fresh out of luck.

With no other options, I decide to sell the only thing I have left. Me. For the very first time. Maybe it'll be okay and the guy will be nice *and* pay me proper cash.

Oh, who am I kidding? I've used up all my lifelines and all I can do now is throw myself at the mercy of Mr Moneybags.

## MILLER

When my cold-hearted father passes, my older brothers get the multi-billion family businesses in the inheritance. I get landed with Dad's secret club and all its complications.

The last thing I need is some little kitten coming to me, asking me for help. But he's so sweet and beautiful, I find myself bending over backwards to fix his problems and save his innocence. Maybe even awaken something new in him.

But the more I see of him, the more I want to be the one to cherish him and protect him from the world.

If only he'd let me before it's too late…

*Nine Lives* is a super steamy, standalone MM gay romance novel featuring first times, a very good baby kitten who gets very naughty for his Daddy in the bedroom, lots of cream, totally rubbish fathers who cause terror even from beyond the grave, an actual cat with matchmaking on her mind, and a guaranteed HEA with absolutely no cliffhanger.

**Click here to get the Nine Lives eBook**

## PINE COVE BOX SET BY HJ WELCH

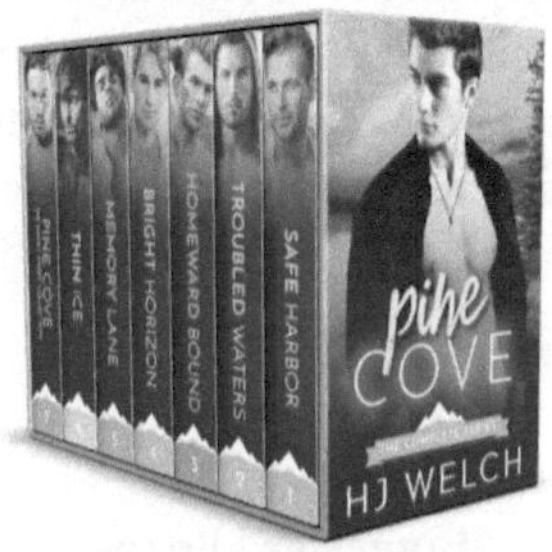

Welcome to Pine Cove, where true love lives happily ever after! **This 2000 page box set contains all six novels as well as all five companion short stories.**

**Click here to get the Pine Cove eBook bundle**

**Click here to get the Pine Cove audio bundle**

———

### Safe Harbor

Robin Coal needs a fake boyfriend for his high school reunion. He asks his housemate: a gorgeous, totally straight ex-Marine. What could go wrong? There's only one bed, and Dair might not be so straight after all... When Robin's past threatens their future, only Dair can save him.

———

***Sweet Spot***

It's Halloween and Robin has prepared a sexy little surprise for his boyfriend Dair when he gets home from work. Hold on to your horses, Marine!

———

### Troubled Waters

Bodyguard Scout Duffy doesn't know what's worse: the fact that his scorching one-night-stand, Emery Klein, is his bratty new client, or the fact that he doesn't even remember Scout. But Emery's life is in danger thanks to his out and proud charity work, and once he finally recognizes Scout, their chemistry in undeniable.

———

### Homeward Bound

Swift Coal just found out he's a father, and his daughter (and her cranky cat) are coming to stay. His best friend's younger brother, Micha Perkins, has nowhere to go and a wrongfully tattered reputation. He's relieved when Swift asks him to be a live-in babysitter. He just has to hide his lifelong crush. Easy, because Swift is straight—right?

———

### Bright Horizon

With sixteen years between them, baker Ben Turner and lawyer Elias Solomon have no idea their crush is mutual. But when Ben inherits his long-lost family's estate and becomes an overnight millionaire, Elias swears to protect the innocent younger man from the vultures circling him. To unravel the mystery of the inheritance, they must go to England to confront Ben's estranged relatives…and their feelings for each other.

———

***Crossed Paths***

Raj Bhat is done living in the shadows. It's time for him to take charge of his own destiny and tell the man he's fallen for how he really feels.

———

***Midnight Sky***

It's the night before New Year's Eve. Taylan Demir is all alone, and he's just lost his dog. Except when his handsome customer, Hudson Perkins, comes to his rescue, Taylan doesn't just get his dog back. He's suddenly got a hot date, and maybe someone to kiss when the clock strikes midnight.

———

**Memory Lane**

Angel Shields saved Jay Coal's life in high school, and Jay has secretly loved his straight best friend ever since. Now Angel's back in town with amnesia after a suspicious work accident and it's Jay's turn to rescue him. He pretends to be Angel's fiancé to see him in the hospital, but with his scrambled-up memory, Angel's not sure it's fictional after all. He just knows he loves Jay more than ever.

———

**Thin Ice**

Kamran's ex broke his heart, tricked him into aiding a bank robbery, and now he wants him to do one last job. There's only one way to say no: seek the protective custody of the biggest, grumpiest FBI agent ever, Lee Marshall. And pretend to be his boyfriend for a week-long family reunion in their giant mansion. Wait, what?

———

***Calm Shores***

Gorgeous, sophisticated Dante walks into Oliver's bar and orders…a boyfriend?! Dante needs a man to keep his mother from setting him back up with his awful, cheating ex, and Oliver is up for the challenge.

———

***Fresh Snow***

Emery Klein is throwing the best Christmas party ever, but his fiancé, Scout Duffy, and all their friends have something more exciting in mind.

———

*Each Pine Cove book can be read as a stand alone and has its own happy ever after. But if you read the whole series, you'll see a lot of familiar faces!*

**Click here to get the Pine Cove eBook bundle**

**Click here to get the Pine Cove audio bundle**

# About the Author

HJ Welch is an author of contemporary MM romance series, including the international bestselling Pine Cove series. She lives just outside of London with her husband and two balls of fluff that occasionally pretend to be cats. She began writing at an early age, later honing her craft online in the world of fanfiction on sites like Wattpad. Fifteen years and over half a million words later, she sought out original MM novels to read. By the end of 2016 she had written her first book of her own, and in 2017 she achieved her lifelong dream of becoming a full-time author. When she's not writing she's usually dancing, singing, filming music videos, taking long walks, working on jigsaw puzzles, drinking prosecco, or talking about Eurovision.

She also writes contemporary British MM fairy tale adaptations as Helen Juliet.

———

You can contact Helen via the following:
Newsletter: https://www.subscribepage.com/helenjuliet
Website – www.hjwelch.com
Facebook Group – Helen's Jewels
Instagram – @helenjwrites
Twitter – @helenjwrites
Book Bub – @HJWelchAuthor
Facebook Page – @HJWelchAuthor

www.ingramcontent.com/pod-product-compliance
Lightning Source LLC
Chambersburg PA
CBHW051222210726
48290CB00003B/758